The Road to Success Is Paved with Failure

Other Books by Joey Green

Hellbent on Insanity

The Unofficial Gilligan's Island Handbook

The Get Smart Handbook

The Partridge Family Album

Polish Your Furniture with Panty Hose

Hi Bob!

Selling Out: If Famous Authors Wrote Advertising

Paint Your House with Powdered Milk

Wash Your Hair with Whipped Cream

The Bubble Wrap Book

Joey Green's Encyclopedia

The Warning Label Book

The Zen of Oz: Ten Spiritual Lessons from Over the Rainbow

Monica Speaks

The Official Slinky Book

You Know You've Reached Middle Age If . . .

The Mad Scientist Handbook

Clean Your Clothes with Cheez Whiz

The Road to Success Is Paved with Failure

Hundreds of famous people who triumphed over inauspicious beginnings, crushing rejections, humiliating defeats, and other speed bumps along life's highway

Joey Green

Little, Brown and Company
Boston   New York   London

First edition

For information on Time Warner Trade Publishing's online publishing
program, visit www.ipublish.com.

ISBN 0-316-64881-7
LCCN 2001087914

10 9 8 7 6 5 4 3 2 1
Q-FF

Book design by Joey Green
Printed in the United States of America

For Ashley and Julia,
who never fail to amaze me

Introduction

If at first you don't succeed, welcome to the club. You'll be delighted to learn that you're in excellent company. Elvis Presley, Marilyn Monroe, John F. Kennedy, the Beatles, Thomas Edison, Madonna, Benjamin Franklin—they all had major failures when they started out.

It all goes to show that failure is simply a minor stumbling block on the road to success. Of course, you might not necessarily be on the right road—but you can always get off at the next exit and ask for directions. Sure, failure can make you bury your head under the covers, sleep till noon, and then lounge around your mobile home in a smelly old bathrobe, taking swigs from a bottle of Southern Comfort to wash down a box of day-old powdered jelly donuts. But failure also builds character, helps you hone your skills, tests your determination, fortifies you with eight essential vitamins, and gives you the inner strength and courage to go back out there and fall flat on your face all over again.

Take pride in your failures—because you can't possibly succeed unless you have the courage to fail. When Thomas Edison's experiments with a storage battery failed to produce any positive results, the inventor refused to concede defeat. "I've just found 10,000 ways that won't work."

Anyone who's anybody has failed, and knowing that can be encouraging and uplifting. And so, as a public service, here are the famous successes who were once failures, losers, drop-outs, flunkies, suckers, saps, schlemiels, and schlemazels. They all looked failure square in the face and spit in its eye. You can too. Just remember, everyone falls down. You're not a failure until you don't get back up.

Marilyn Monroe was
dropped in 1947 by
Twentieth Century-Fox
after one year under contract
because production chief
Darryl Zanuck thought
she was unattractive.

Marilyn Monroe became a Hollywood sex goddess, starring in
*All About Eve, Gentlemen Prefer Blondes, The Seven Year Itch,
Some Like It Hot,* and *The Misfits.*

Dr. Seuss's first book,
*And to Think That I Saw
It on Mulberry Street*,
was rejected by twenty-seven
publishing houses, and
Seuss considered burning
the manuscript.

———

Dr. Seuss became the author of more than forty best-selling children's books, including *The Cat in the Hat, Green Eggs and Ham, Horton the Elephant, How the Grinch Stole Christmas*, and *The 500 Hats of Bartholomew Cubbins*.

Cary Grant was called to the stage during an assembly in 1918 and publicly expelled from Fairfield Secondary School for sneaking into the girls lavatory.

Cary Grant became a leading man in movies, starring in more than seventy films, most notably *Topper, Bringing Up Baby, Gunga Din, The Philadelphia Story*, and *North by Northwest*.

Barbra Streisand made her stage debut at age nineteen in 1961 in the off-Broadway revue *Another Evening with Harry Stoones*. The show opened and closed in a single night.

Barbra Streisand became the top-selling female recording artist in the world and starred in the films *Funny Girl, Hello Dolly!, The Way We Were, A Star Is Born,* and *Yentl.*

Peter Benchley was fired as a speech writer for Richard Nixon.

Peter Benchley went on to write the best-selling novel *Jaws*, selling the movie rights before the book was even published.

Diana Spencer worked as a kindergarten teacher's aide.

Lady Diana Spencer became the Princess of Wales when she married Prince Charles in 1981.

Frank Sinatra was expelled from high school after just forty-seven days for his rowdy behavior.

Frank Sinatra became a superstar as an actor and singer, one of the wealthiest men in show business, and leader of the Rat Pack. He starred in the films *From Here to Eternity, Guys and Dolls, The Manchurian Candidate,* and *Von Ryan's Express.*

Kurt Vonnegut, Jr., serving in the U.S. Army during World War II, was captured by the Germans and imprisoned in Dresden, Germany.

Kurt Vonnegut, Jr., wrote about that experience in his novel *Slaughterhouse-Five,* which became a best-seller and was made into a hit movie. Vonnegut's other novels include *Cat's Cradle, Breakfast of Champions,* and *Jailbird.*

15

Tom Cruise
auditioned for a role on the
television version of *Fame*,
but the casting director told him
he wasn't "pretty enough."

Tom Cruise went on to become the heartthrob of millions of
women as the star of the films *Risky Business, Top Gun,
Rain Man, A Few Good Men*, and *Jerry McGuire*.

Ulysses S. Grant failed as a farmer, a real estate agent, a U.S. Customs official, and a store clerk.

Ulysses S. Grant commanded the Union armies during the Civil War and was elected 18th president of the United States in 1868.

Ryan O'Neal spent fifty-one days in jail as a teenager for assault and battery during a New Year's Eve party.

Ryan O'Neal was nominated for an Academy Award for his role in *Love Story*. He starred in the films *What's Up, Doc?*, *Paper Moon*, and *A Bridge Too Far*.

Joan of Arc was illiterate.

Joan of Arc, a French national heroine and beloved saint of the Roman Catholic Church, liberated the besieged city of Orléans from the English in 1429 and escorted the uncrowned King Charles VII to the city of Reims for his coronation.

Michael Jordan was cut from his high school's varsity football team as a sophomore.

Michael Jordan became one of the greatest basketball players in the history of the sport.

Edgar Allan Poe was
expelled from West Point
for "gross neglect of duty"
and "disobedience of orders."
His early poems met with
no success.

Edgar Allan Poe became one of America's greatest poets,
short-story writers, and literary critics. He wrote "The Raven,"
"The Murders in the Rue Morgue," "The Fall of the House of
Usher," "The Black Cat," and "The Pit and the Pendulum."

Rock Hudson required thirty-eight takes before he could successfully complete one line in his first movie, *Fighter Squadron.*

Rock Hudson went on to be nominated for an Academy Award for his role in *Giant*, act in bedroom comedies opposite Doris Day, and star in the television series *McMillan and Wife.*

Humphrey Bogart, dropped by Twentieth Century-Fox in 1931 after appearing in six mediocre movies, returned to New York, where he was fired from a job reading radio playlets for laxatives. He then earned a living playing chess for fifty cents a round.

Humphrey Bogart became a top box-office attraction in movies and won an Academy Award for his role in *The African Queen*. He starred in *The Petrified Forest, The Maltese Falcon, Casablanca, The Treasure of Sierra Madre*, and *Key Largo*.

Dr. Ruth Westheimer never completed high school, had two failed marriages, and worked as a housemaid.

Dr. Ruth Westheimer became a sex expert on radio and television and the author of the best-selling book *Good Sex*.

Johnny Cash sold electrical appliances door to door.

Johnny Cash became a country music superstar, won ten Grammy Awards, sold more than fifty million albums, sang the hit songs "Folsom Prison Blues," "Ring of Fire," and "I Walk the Line," and hosted *The Johnny Cash Show* on television.

O. Henry, falsely accused of embezzling from a bank, fled to Honduras and, upon his return to his wife's deathbed in Austin, Texas, was arrested and imprisoned for three years.

O. Henry wrote and published several short stories while in jail and after his release became one of the most famous short-story writers of his day. Among his 250 works of fiction, his best-known story is "The Gift of the Magi."

Sigmund Freud's first book, *The Interpretation of Dreams,* sold only 600 copies and netted the author a mere $250 in royalties in the first eight years after its publication.

Sigmund Freud became the father of psychoanalysis and one of the most influential thinkers of the twentieth century. His most widely read book, *The Interpretation of Dreams*, is considered the gospel of psychoanalysis.

Helen Gurley Brown dropped out of a Texas college after only one semester due to lack of finances, then worked in nineteen different secretarial jobs over the next eight years.

Helen Gurley Brown wrote the best-seller *Sex and the Single Girl* and served as editor-in-chief of *Cosmopolitan* magazine.

Yul Brynner was grounded as a trapeze artist with the Paris Cirque d'Hiver after nearly being crippled by a fall.

Yul Brynner won the Academy Award for Best Actor for his role as the king in *The King and I.* His other films include *The Ten Commandments, The Brothers Karamazov, The Magnificent Seven, Cast a Giant Shadow,* and *Westworld.*

Walt Disney's first cartoon production company, Laugh-O-Gram, went bankrupt.

Walt Disney created Mickey Mouse and became the most famous name in film animation. He produced *Snow White and the Seven Dwarfs, Pinocchio, Fantasia, Bambi*, and *Cinderella*, and founded Disneyland.

Carroll O'Connor auditioned for the role of the Skipper on *Gilligan's Island* but lost the part to Alan Hale, Jr.

Carroll O'Connor went on to gain worldwide fame as Archie Bunker on the television series *All in the Family* and starred as Chief Bill Gillespie on *In the Heat of the Night*, winning Emmy Awards for both roles.

Cyndi Lauper lost her voice after intense vocal training in 1977, prompting doctors to say she would never sing again.

Cyndi Lauper regained her voice and recorded the hit rock 'n' roll albums *She's So Unusual* and *True Colors*, won the 1984 Grammy Award for Best New Artist, and recorded the hit songs "Girls Just Want to Have Fun" and "Time After Time."

Martin Luther was excommunicated by Pope Leo X for nailing his *Ninety-Five Theses* to the door of the Castle Church at Wittenberg.

Martin Luther went on to lead the Reformation in Germany, giving birth to Protestantism. His translation of the Bible into German is considered a literary masterpiece.

Burt Reynolds's first television series, *Dan August*, was canceled in 1971 after just one season. He then appeared as a bachelor on *The Dating Game* and wasn't chosen.

———————

Burt Reynolds became a leading man and sex symbol in Hollywood, starring in *Deliverance, The Man Who Loved Cat Dancing, The Longest Yard,* and *Smokey and the Bandit*. He appeared as the first-ever nude male centerfold in *Cosmopolitan* in April 1972 and starred in the television series *Evening Shade*.

David Letterman was a regular on *The Starland Vocal Band Show* (canceled by CBS after three months in 1977), a regular on Mary Tyler Moore's television comedy variety series, *Mary* (canceled by CBS after only three telecasts in 1978), and the host of *The David Letterman Show*, a national morning talk show (canceled by CBS after just a few months in 1980).

David Letterman became the Emmy Award–winning host of *Late Night with David Letterman* on NBC and *The Late Show* on CBS.

Colleen Dewhurst dropped out of Downer College for Young Ladies (now Laurence University) and worked as an elevator operator and a gym instructor.

Colleen Dewhurst became one of the leading ladies of the New York stage, winning Tony Awards for *All the Way Home* and *A Moon for the Misbegotten* on Broadway.

Theodore Roosevelt ran in 1886 as the Republican candidate for mayor of New York City —and lost.

Theodore Roosevelt served two years as governor of New York, was elected vice president of the United States under William McKinley, became president upon McKinley's assassination, and was elected to a full term as president in 1904. His face is carved into Mount Rushmore.

The Beatles were rejected
in 1962 by Decca Records executive
Dick Rowe, who signed Brian Poole &
The Tremeloes instead, following
back-to-back auditions by both
groups. The Beatles' Decca audition
tape was subsequently turned down
by Pey, Philips, Columbia, and HMV.

The Beatles, finally offered a recording contract by Parlophone
producer George Martin, became the most influential rock 'n' roll
group in history.

Charles Lindbergh dropped out of the University of Wisconsin in his sophomore year.

Charles Lindbergh became the first person to fly solo, nonstop across the Atlantic Ocean, received a Congressional Medal of Honor from President Calvin Coolidge, and won a Pulitzer Prize in 1954 for his account of his historic 1927 flight.

Martin Luther King, Jr., was forced at age fourteen to surrender his bus seat to a white passenger and stand for the next ninety miles.

Martin Luther King, Jr., became leader of the American civil rights movement, delivered his famous "I Have a Dream" speech on the steps of the Lincoln Memorial before an audience of more than 200,000 people in 1963, and was awarded the Nobel Peace Prize in 1964.

Richard Dreyfuss dropped out of San Fernando Valley State College after his freshman year.

Richard Dreyfuss won an Academy Award as Best Actor for *The Goodbye Girl*. He starred in *American Graffiti*, *Jaws*, *Close Encounters of the Third Kind*, and *Mr. Holland's Opus*.

Pat Benatar dropped out of Juilliard School of Music, worked as a bank clerk and a waitress, and was rejected by several major record labels.

Pat Benatar became a rock 'n' roll star, recorded the hit singles "Hit Me with Your Best Shot" and "Love Is a Battlefield," and won Grammy Awards for her albums *Crime of Passion* and *Precious Time* and her hit single "Fire and Ice."

Charles Conrad flunked out of Haverford, a prestigious private boys school in Pennsylvania, where he was known as a prankster who hid in drainpipes and blew up Bunsen burners in the science lab.

In 1969, as commander of Apollo 12, Charles Conrad became the third astronaut to walk on the moon.

George Lucas's first film, *THX-1138*, flopped in 1971, prompting every major studio to turn down his next movie project, *American Graffiti.*

Universal finally agreed to back *American Graffiti*, but only after George Lucas brought Francis Ford Coppola aboard as producer. Lucas went on to produce the highly successful *Star Wars* movies.

Adlai Stevenson at age twelve accidentally fired an old .22 rifle during a Christmas party at his home, killing one of the female guests.

Adlai Stevenson became the governor of Illinois, the Democratic candidate for president of the United States in 1952 and 1956, and the U.S. Ambassador to the United Nations.

Jane Fonda was kicked out of the Girl Scouts for telling dirty jokes.

Jane Fonda starred in the films *Cat Ballou, Klute, Coming Home, The China Syndrome*, and *On Golden Pond*. She was an outspoken political activist against the Vietnam war and launched a fitness revolution in 1982 when she released her first work-out video.

Bruce Springsteen was stuffed into a garbage can by a nun when he was in the third grade "because she told me that's where I belonged." Springsteen's first album, *Greetings from Asbury Park,* released in 1973, initially sold only 25,000 copies, and the accompanying single, "Blinded by the Light," never made the charts.

With the release of his third album, *Born to Run*, in 1975, Bruce Springsteen was featured on the covers of both *Time* and *Newsweek* in the same week, igniting sales of his first two albums and turning "The Boss" into a rock 'n' roll legend.

Judy Garland performed with her two older sisters in the "Gumm Sisters Kiddie Act," but the act never achieved major success and broke up when one of the sisters married.

Judy Garland won an Academy Award for her role as Dorothy in *The Wizard of Oz* and became a world-famous singer. She starred in the Andy Hardy movies with Mickey Rooney, and in *For Me and My Gal, Meet Me in St. Louis, The Clock*, and *A Star Is Born*.

Karl Marx, after obtaining his doctorate in philosophy from the university in Jena, Prussia, in 1841, was denied a job as a teacher at the university because he opposed the Prussian government.

Karl Marx went on to write *The Communist Manifesto* with Friedrich Engels and *Das Kapital*. He founded two of the most powerful mass movements in history—democratic socialism and revolutionary communism.

Jonathan Swift was censured at Trinity College for "offenses against discipline" and obtained his degree only by "special grace."

Jonathan Swift, considered one of the world's greatest satirists, wrote *A Tale of a Tub, Gulliver's Travels,* and "A Modest Proposal."

Goldie Hawn dropped out of American University at age eighteen and worked as a go-go dancer at the New York discotheque Dudes 'n' Dolls.

Goldie Hawn was a regular on the television variety show *Rowan & Martin's Laugh-In*, won an Academy Award for Best Supporting Actress for her role in the movie *Cactus Flower*, and starred in *Sugarland Express, Butterflies Are Free, Shampoo, Foul Play*, and *Private Benjamin* (which she also executive produced).

Bill Clinton, having served one term as governor of Arkansas, lost his bid for re-election in 1980.

Bill Clinton was re-elected governor of Arkansas in 1982, 1984, 1986, and 1990, elected 42nd president of the United States in 1992, and re-elected in 1996. He survived an impeachment trial in 1998.

Axl Rose and Izzy Stradlin earned eight dollars an hour smoking cigarettes as part of a scientific study at UCLA.

Axl Rose and Izzy Stradlin founded the heavy metal group Guns N' Roses, best known for their album *Appetite for Destruction*, including the hit song "Sweet Child O' Mine."

Greta Garbo grew up in poverty in Stockholm's shabbiest district, quit school at thirteen, and worked as a lather girl in a barbershop.

Greta Garbo became a Hollywood legend, starring in *Temptress*, *Anna Christie*, *Mata Hari*, *Grand Hotel*, and *Anna Karenina*.

Orville Wright was expelled from the sixth grade for "mischievous behavior."

Orville Wright went on to invent the world's first power-driven airplane with his brother Wilbur in 1903.

James Cagney worked as a female impersonator in a revue in Yorkville, New York.

James Cagney won the Academy Award for Best Actor for his role as George M. Cohan in *Yankee Doodle Dandy*. His films include such classics as *Man of a Thousand Faces*, *The Public Enemy*, *Angels with Dirty Faces*, *Mister Roberts*, and *One, Two, Three*.

Jerry Seinfeld sold lightbulbs over the telephone and peddled fake jewelry on the street.

Jerry Seinfeld starred in the hit sitcom *Seinfeld*, one of the most popular American television series of all time.

Courtney Love was sent to reform school for stealing a Kiss T-shirt from Woolworth's.

Courtney Love became lead singer of Hole, an abrasive alternative rock band best known for their gold album *Live Through This,* and starred in the movie *The People vs. Larry Flynt.*

Chrissie Hynde dropped out of Kent State University and went to London, where she worked in Malcolm McLaren's Sex boutique.

Chrissie Hynde became lead singer of the Pretenders, best known for their top ten album *Learning to Crawl* and their hit songs "Middle of the Road," "Back on the Chain Gang," and "My City Was Gone."

John Denver threw a party to celebrate the publication of his high school yearbook and no one showed up.

John Denver became an internationally famous recording star, best remembered for his pop ballads "Sunshine on My Shoulder" and "Rocky Mountain High," and starred in the movie *Oh God!*

Charlotte Brontë's first novel, *The Professor,* was rejected by several publishers and wasn't printed until 1857— two years after her death.

Charlotte Brontë is the author of the classic novel *Jane Eyre*.

Andy Warhol, a sickly child
whose white skin was marred
by brown blotches and acne,
was nicknamed "Spot," "Albino,"
and "Andy the Red-Nosed Warhol"
by other kids and had
three nervous breakdowns.

Andy Warhol became a pop artist famous for his vivid silk-screen prints of Campbell's soup cans and Marilyn Monroe's face. He founded and edited *Interview* magazine and predicted that one day everyone would get fifteen minutes of fame.

Bill Gates dropped out of Harvard University in 1975.

That same year, Bill Gates formed Microsoft Corporation with Paul Allen. Gates designed the software to run the first micro-computers and became the world's richest man.

Jesse Owens worked as an elevator operator.

Jesse Owens became a track star, set three world records in 1935, and won three gold medals at the 1936 Olympic Games in Berlin.

Nick Nolte was arrested in 1962 for counterfeiting draft cards and was sentenced to five years' probation.

Nick Nolte went on to star in the films *The Deep*, *48 Hours*, *Down and Out in Beverly Hills*, *The Prince of Tides*, and *Three Fugitives*.

Christopher Columbus miscalculated the size of the globe and the width of the Atlantic Ocean and wound up discovering the island of San Salvador in the Bahamas (which he believed to be an island of the Indies), Cuba (which he thought to be a part of China), and the Dominican Republic (which he also mistook as part of the Far East).

———

Christopher Columbus made three more voyages to the New World, eventually discovering South America and Central America.

Deborah Harry worked as a beautician and a Playboy bunny.

Deborah Harry became the lead singer of Blondie, best known for their albums *Parallel Lines* and *Eat to the Beat* and their hit singles "One Way or Another," "Rapture," and "The Tide Is High."

Jack Nicholson worked as an office boy at MGM's cartoon department and appeared in several low-budget Roger Corman horror movies. He co-wrote and co-produced the movie *Head,* starring the Monkees, which bombed at the box office.

Jack Nicholson won Academy Awards for *One Flew Over the Cuckoo's Nest* and *As Good As It Gets*. He also starred in *Easy Rider, Five Easy Pieces, Chinatown, The Shining,* and *A Few Good Men*.

Tom Waits dropped out of high school at age sixteen to work at Napoleon's Pizza House.

Tom Waits became a singer-songwriter known for his raspy voice
and his hit albums *Swordfishtrombones* and *Bone Machine*.
He also starred in the movies *Down by Law* and *Rumble Fish*.

Mao Tse-tung, passed over for a promotion, quit his job in 1918 as an assistant to the chief librarian of the University of Beijing.

Mao Tse-tung became Chairman of the Communist Party in China, led the Chinese revolution, and became ruler of the People's Republic of China from 1949 to 1976.

Gloria Estefan worked as a Spanish and French interpreter at Miami International Airport.

Gloria Estefan became the lead singer of the Miami Sound Machine, famous for their album *Let It Loose* and their hit songs "Anything for You," "Words Get in the Way," and "Rhythm Is Gonna Get You."

Sylvester Stallone, thrown out of fourteen schools in eleven years, studied drama at the University of Miami, where professors discouraged him from pursuing a career in acting. After starring in porn films, Stallone auditioned unsuccessfully for roles in *Dog Day Afternoon, Serpico,* and *The Godfather.*

Sylvester Stallone went on to write and star in the box-office hit *Rocky*, nominated for the Academy Award for Best Actor and Best Screenplay. The film established Stallone as one of Hollywood's leading men.

Cecil B. DeMille ran away from Pennsylvania Military College to enlist in the army to fight in the Spanish-American War but was turned down because he was underage.

Cecil B. DeMille became a Hollywood producer and director famous for film spectaculars, including *The Ten Commandments, The King of Kings, Cleopatra, The Crusades,* and *The Greatest Show on Earth.*

Regis Philbin was fired from his job as a stagehand at KCOP-TV in San Diego, California.

Regis Philbin became the host of the popular television talk show
Live with Regis and Kathy Lee and the television game show
Who Wants to Be a Millionaire?

Natalie Cole, a former heroin addict, was rejected by nearly all of the major recording companies.

Natalie Cole won a Grammy Award for her number-one album *Unforgettable with Love*, which features a duet with her deceased father, pop legend Nat "King" Cole, created through digital engineering.

Robin Williams was a cast member
of *The Richard Pryor Show*
(which was canceled
after five episodes in 1977)
and a regular on the 1978 version
of *Laugh-In* (which was canceled
after one season).

Robin Williams went on to star in the comedy smash
Mork & Mindy and won an Academy Award for *Good Will Hunting*.
He also starred in *Moscow on the Hudson, Dead Poets Society,
Good Morning, Vietnam,* and *Patch Adams.*

Chuck Berry was convicted of armed robbery and spent three years in the Algoa Reform School in Missouri. After his release, he worked as a hairdresser.

Chuck Berry became a dominant force in the evolution of rock 'n' roll. His hits include "Maybellene," "Roll Over Beethoven," "No Particular Place to Go," and "Johnny B. Goode."

Gamal Abdel Nasser
was expelled from
secondary school for
taking part in a demonstration
against the British, who
controlled Egypt at the time.
He later dropped out of
law school.

Gamal Abdel Nasser was elected president of Egypt in 1956.

Billy Joel, embarrassed by
his first album, *Cold Spring Harbor*,
spent six months playing bar piano
in the lounge of the
Executive Room in Los Angeles,
under the pseudonym Bill Martin.

———

Billy Joel became a rock legend with his albums *Piano Man, Streetlife Serenade, The Stranger,* and *Glass Houses*. His hit songs include "Just the Way You Are," "You May Be Right," "It's Still Rock and Roll to Me," "Tell Her About It," and "Uptown Girl."

James Earl Jones waxed floors for a living.

James Earl Jones, the voice of Darth Vader in the *Star Wars* films, appeared in *Dr. Strangelove, Coming to America, The Hunt for Red October, The Great White Hope,* and *Field of Dreams.*

Myrna Loy failed her first screen test, given by Rudolph Valentino.

Myrna Loy became Hollywood's number-one female box-office attraction, co-starring with William Powell in the *Thin Man* films and starring in *The Best Years of Our Lives, The Bachelor and the Bobby-Soxer,* and *Mr. Blandings Builds His Dream House.*

Dashiell Hammett dropped out of school at age thirteen to become a messenger boy.

Dashiell Hammett went on to write the best-selling novels *The Maltese Falcon* and *The Thin Man*, which were both made into major hit movies.

Sonny Bono worked on an assembly line at the Douglas Aircraft factory in Los Angeles.

Sonny Bono teamed up with Cher to become the singing duo Sonny and Cher. They starred in their own television variety series and recorded the hit songs "The Beat Goes On" and "I've Got You, Babe."

Sydney Greenstreet went to Ceylon at age eighteen to seek his fortune as a tea planter but was forced out of business by a drought and returned to England.

Sydney Greenstreet became one of the greatest movie villains of all time, starring in *The Maltese Falcon*, *Casablanca*, *Passage to Marseille*, *The Hucksters*, and *Flamingo Road*.

Andrew Carnegie worked as a bobbin boy in a cotton factory for $1.20 a week.

Andrew Carnegie became one of the richest men in the world and one of the greatest philanthropists, supporting education, public libraries, and the world peace movement.

Henry Fonda dropped out of the University of Minnesota after two years and worked as an office boy at an Omaha credit company.

Henry Fonda starred in more than eighty movies, most notably *The Grapes of Wrath, Mister Roberts, The Wrong Man, 12 Angry Men, The Longest Day, Fail Safe,* and *On Golden Pond,* for which he won an Academy Award.

Jane Russell worked as a receptionist for a chiropodist.

Jane Russell became a Hollywood sex symbol, starring in
The Outlaw and *Gentlemen Prefer Blondes*.

Jack Lemmon played piano in a New York City beer hall.

Jack Lemmon won Academy Awards for his roles in *Mister Roberts*
and *Save the Tiger*. He starred in *Some Like It Hot*, *The Fortune
Cookie*, *The Odd Couple*, *The Out-of-Towners*, and *Grumpy Old Men*.

Jane Austen's first novel, *First Impressions*, was rejected by a publisher in 1797. Her second novel, *Northanger Abbey*, was sold in 1803 to a publisher who never published it.

Jane Austen revised *First Impressions*, retitled it *Pride and Prejudice,* and sold it to a publisher who printed it in 1813. Her other novels include *Sense and Sensibility, Emma,* and *Persuasion. Northanger Abbey* was published in 1818, a year after her death.

Kirk Douglas worked as a waiter, wrestled professionally, then worked as an usher and a bellhop.

Kirk Douglas became a leading man in Hollywood movies, starring in *20,000 Leagues Under the Sea*, *Gunfight at the O.K. Corral*, *Spartacus*, *Cast a Giant Shadow*, and *There Was a Crooked Man*.

Carly Fiorina, a UCLA law school dropout, worked as a Hewlett-Packard shipping clerk.

Carly Fiorina, appointed chief executive officer of
Hewlett-Packard in 1999, became the first female chief executive
of a blue-chip company.

George Washington wanted to become a sailor in the British Royal Navy at age fourteen, but his mother refused to let him join. At twenty, he proposed marriage at least twice to sixteen-year-old Betsy Fauntleroy, but she repeatedly spurned him.

George Washington married Martha Custis in 1759, was elected Commander in Chief of the U.S. Military in 1775, and was elected first president of the United States in 1789.

Elvis Presley's music teacher at L.C. Humes High School in Memphis, Tennessee, gave him a C and told him he couldn't sing.

Elvis Presley became "the king of rock 'n' roll," selling more than 600 million albums and singles before his death in 1977. He starred in thirty-three movies, including *Love Me Tender*, *Jailhouse Rock*, and *Girl Happy*.

Jackie Gleason dropped out of high school before completing the ninth grade, hustled pool bets, and worked as a carnival barker at an auto stunt show.

Jackie Gleason went on to star as Ralph Kramden in the classic television series *The Honeymooners*.

90

Jay Leno applied for a job at Woolworth's but failed the employment test.

Jay Leno became a popular comedian and then Johnny Carson's successor as host of *The Tonight Show*..

Francis Bacon was convicted of bribery and imprisoned in the Tower of London.

Francis Bacon dedicated the rest of his life to literary and philosophical work, became the father of modern empiricism, and was described by Alexander Pope as "the wisest, brightest, meanest of mankind."

Ozzy Osbourne served two months in Winson Green prison for burglary at age seventeen and was fired from a job in a slaughterhouse.

Ozzy Osbourne formed the legendary heavy metal band Black Sabbath, known for their songs "Paranoid" and "Iron Man," and launched a solo career in 1977, releasing the albums *Diary of a Madman*, *Blizzard of Oz*, and *No More Tears*.

Samuel Johnson dropped out of Oxford in 1729 after fourteen months and never received a degree. In 1735, he founded a private school in Edial, which went out of business within two years, prompting Johnson to move to London, nearly penniless.

Samuel Johnson became the greatest English writer of his day, best known for his poem "The Vanity of Human Wishes" and his books *London, Dictionary of the English Language,* and *Rasselas, Prince of Abyssinia.*

Billy Crystal was selected as an original cast member of *Saturday Night Live* but was cut from the cast before the show's premiere.

Billy Crystal went on to star as Jodie Dallas on the sitcom *Soap*, became a cast member of *Saturday Night Live* in the 1984-1985 season, and starred in the films *Throw Mama from the Train*, *When Harry Met Sally*, and *City Slickers*.

Gary Cooper moved to Los Angeles to seek work as a political cartoonist but wound up as a door-to-door salesman.

Gary Cooper became one of Hollywood's greatest stars, winning two Academy Awards as Best Actor for *Sergeant York* and *High Noon*. He was the strong, silent hero of *Mr. Deeds Goes to Town*, *Beau Geste*, *Meet John Doe*, *The Pride of the Yankees*, *For Whom the Bell Tolls*, and *The Fountainhead*.

Geri Halliwell worked as a hair-dresser, nude model, and game-show hostess on Turkish television; Melanie Chisholm worked in a fish-and-chips shop in England; and Emma Bunton auditioned for the part of Bianca in the British television series *EastEnders* but failed to get the part.

Geri Halliwell, Melanie Chisholm, and Emma Bunton became Ginger Spice, Sporty Spice, and Baby Spice of the Spice Girls, singing in the highest-grossing concert tour and on the top-selling album of 1998.

Jimmy Carter played hooky
from high school as an
April Fool's joke
to go to a movie with friends.
The principal paddled Carter
and denied him the right to
graduate as class valedictorian.

Jimmy Carter married another class valedictorian, Rosalynn Smith,
and was elected governor of Georgia in 1970 and the 39th
president of the United States in 1976.

Barbara Walters was told in 1957 by Don Hewitt, who became executive producer of *60 Minutes*, to "stay out of television."

Barbara Walters became a host on the television talk show *Today,* an anchorwoman on *The ABC Evening News,* and a host of *20/20.* She has won six Emmy Awards for her work on television and was elected in 1990 to the Television Hall of Fame.

Joseph bragged to his ten older brothers about his dreams of future power, prompting them to throw him into a pit and sell him to Ishmaelite traders.

Joseph, according to the biblical book of Genesis, interpreted the dreams of the Egyptian pharaoh, who then appointed him second-in-command.

Jack Benny was expelled from high school in Waukegan, Illinois, after flunking his exams.

Jack Benny became one of America's favorite comedians, starring
as a violin-playing miser who was eternally thirty-nine on
The Jack Benny Program, first on radio, then on television.
Benny starred in *Charley's Aunt, To Be or Not to Be,
George Washington Slept Here*, and *The Horn Blows at Midnight*.

Nelson Mandela was imprisoned on Robben Island for twenty-seven years as punishment for his efforts opposing apartheid.

Nelson Mandela became South Africa's first democratically elected president in 1994 after sharing the Nobel Peace Prize with his predecessor, F. W. DeClerk, in 1993.

Julie Andrews, having created
the part of Eliza Doolittle
in the Broadway smash hit
My Fair Lady, lost the part
in the movie version
to Audrey Hepburn.

Instead, Julie Andrews made her film debut in Walt Disney's
Mary Poppins, winning the Academy Award for Best Actress.
The following year, she starred in *The Sound of Music,* one of
the top-grossing movies of all time.

103

Noel Gallagher was sentenced to six months' probation for robbing a store in Manchester, England, at age thirteen.

Noel Gallagher and his brother Liam went on to form the rock 'n' roll band Oasis, one of Britain's most popular and critically acclaimed bands, best known for their gold album *Definitely Maybe* and the hit single "Some Might Say."

Marlon Brando threw strings of firecrackers into classrooms at Libertyville High School and hung a dead skunk on the football scoreboard, prompting the principal to tell him, "You'll never do anything but dig ditches." He was later expelled from Shattuck Military Academy in Minnesota for insubordination.

Marlon Brando became a Hollywood legend, representing the nonconforming rebel of the beat generation, and won Academy Awards for his performances in *On the Waterfront* and *The Godfather* (which he turned down to protest the plight of the American Indian). He also starred in *A Streetcar Named Desire*, *The Wild One*, *Last Tango in Paris*, and *Apocalypse Now*.

Leon Trotsky was expelled from the second grade for howling at a teacher who was treating a German student unfairly.

Trotsky became a leader of the Bolshevik revolution and the second-most-powerful man in Russia.

David Cassidy worked in the mailroom of a textile company and landed a role in the Broadway play *The Fig Leaves Are Falling,* which flopped.

David Cassidy became a teen idol as Keith Partridge in the television show *The Partridge Family,* was featured on the cover of *16 Magazine* for twenty-four issues in a row, and performed several concert tours.

Cliff Robertson
auditioned unsuccessfully
for roles in *The Hustler*
(losing to Paul Newman) and
Days of Wine and Roses
(losing to Jack Lemmon).

Cliff Robertson then optioned the rights to a short story
by Daniel Keyes entitled "Flowers for Algernon" and recruited
Stirling Silliphant to write the screenplay. The resulting movie,
Charly, won Robertson an Academy Award for Best Actor.

Andrew Jackson inherited 300 English pounds, a substantial amount of money for a teenager in 1782, but lost the money gambling on horse races and cockfights. In 1824, Jackson ran for president of the United States but lost to John Quincy Adams.

Four years later, Andrew Jackson beat John Quincy Adams and was elected seventh president of the United States. He was re-elected in 1832.

Dylan Thomas was frequently stuffed butt-first into a wastebasket in grammar school by older boys.

Dylan Thomas went on to become one of the most stirring writers in modern literature as the author of the poem "Do Not Go Gentle into That Good Night," the story collection *Portrait of the Artist as a Young Dog,* and the radio play *Under Milk Wood.*

Cindy Williams worked the midnight shift at a pancake house.

Cindy Williams starred in the movie *American Graffiti* and as Shirley Feeney in the hit sitcom *Laverne and Shirley*.

Jacob, failing to check under the bridal veil at his wedding, married Leah instead of her younger sister Rachel as planned.

According to the biblical book of Genesis,
Jacob eventually married Rachel, and their twelve sons
founded the Twelve Tribes of Israel.

Satchel Paige was placed in the Alabama Reform School for Boys at age twelve for throwing rocks at windows and at boys from rival gangs.

Satchel Paige became one of the greatest pitchers in baseball history and the first black pitcher in the American League.

Jules Verne, having written a
full-length play at age sixteen,
gathered friends and family together
to read his work to them.
The audience's unexpected laughter
prompted Verne to stop reading
after the first act and later
burn the script.

Jules Verne became one of the first science fiction novelists and
wrote *20,000 Leagues Under the Sea, Around the World
in Eighty Days,* and *A Journey to the Center of the Earth.*
He predicted the invention of airplanes, submarines,
television, guided missiles, and space satellites.

Clint Eastwood,
after starring in the horror film
Revenge of the Creature and the
talking-horse movie *Francis in the
Navy,* was fired from Universal by a
studio executive who told him he
spoke too slowly and his Adam's apple
stuck out too far.

Clint Eastwood went on to star as Rowdy Yates in *Rawhide* and became a Hollywood movie legend as the star of *The Good, the Bad and the Ugly, Dirty Harry, Magnum Force,* and *Unforgiven.*

James Fenimore Cooper was expelled from Yale University in his junior year for pulling a series of pranks. His first novel, *Precaution*, received little critical praise.

James Fenimore Cooper became the first American author to achieve worldwide fame. He wrote *The Longstocking Tales,* which includes his masterpiece, *The Last of the Mohicans.*

Betty Grable was told by a ballet teacher to give up the idea of ever becoming a dancer.

Betty Grable became known for her shapely legs and dancing in extravagant musical films, was the GIs' number-one pinup girl during World War II, and starred in *The Gay Divorcee, Moon Over Miami,* and *How to Marry a Millionaire.* Twentieth Century-Fox insured her legs with Lloyd's of London for a million dollars.

Confucius failed to convince the ruler of his own city-state of Lu, China, to make his teachings the official state philosophy. He then traveled to neighboring states, only to have his doctrines rejected by every ruler he visited.

———

Confucius became revered as the most influential and respected philosopher in China's history.

Garth Brooks worked as a bouncer at Tumbleweeds, a nightclub in Stillwater, Oklahoma.

Garth Brooks became a world-renowned country singer, selling more than 95 million albums in the United States alone. His hit songs include "If Tomorrow Never Comes," "The Dance," and "Friends in Low Places."

Erle Stanley Gardner was suspended from high school for drawing a cartoon of the principal on a school wall.

Erle Stanley Gardner went on to practice law for twenty years, create the fictional lawyer Perry Mason and the successful television series based on his exploits, and write 129 detective novels that sold more than 300 million books worldwide.

Lucille Ball moved to New York at age fifteen and enrolled in John Murray Anderson's drama school, where she was repeatedly told that she had no talent and should return home. Failing to get into any Broadway chorus lines, she worked as a waitress and a soda jerk in a Broadway drugstore.

━━━━━━━

Lucille Ball became the star of one of the most successful comedy shows in television history, *I Love Lucy,* ran Desilu Productions, and won four Emmy Awards. She also starred in more than sixty movies.

Feodor Dostoyevsky was sentenced to four years of hard labor in Siberia for alleged revolutionary activity.

Feodor Dostoyevsky went on to detail his prison life in his novel *Memoirs from the House of the Dead,* then wrote *Crime and Punishment, The Idiot, The Possessed,* and *The Brothers Karamazov.* He is considered one of Russia's greatest novelists.

David Crosby auditioned for *The Monkees* but lost the part because he had "bad teeth."

David Crosby became a rock 'n' roll legend, played for the Byrds and the supergroup Crosby, Stills, Nash, and Young, and wrote the hit songs "Eight Miles High," "Dèjá Vu," and "Long Time Gone."

Fidel Castro was sentenced
to fifteen years in prison
for attempting to stage
a revolution against Cuba's
Batista government in 1953.
When Batista released him two
years later, Castro went into
exile in Mexico.

Fidel Castro overthrew the military dictatorship of Fulgencio
Batista in 1959 and became the Communist dictator of Cuba.

Muddy Waters earned a living driving a truck for a venetian-blind manufacturer in Mississippi.

Muddy Waters became the kingpin of the Chicago blues scene and a legend in the history of blues music with his hit songs "Rollin' Stone," "Louisiana Blues," "She Moves Me," "I'm You're Hoochie Coochie Man," and "I'm Ready."

William Goldman was fired after writing his first screenplay, for the movie *Charly*. A new screenwriter was hired to write the script from scratch.

━━━━━━━

William Goldman went on to write the screenplays for
*Butch Cassidy and the Sundance Kid, The Stepford Wives,
All the President's Men, Marathon Man,* and *A Bridge Too Far*.
He won two Academy Awards for Best Screenplay.

Franklin Delano Roosevelt ran for vice president of the United States in 1920 on the Democratic ticket with presidential candidate James M. Cox. They lost to Warren G. Harding and Calvin Coolidge. The following year, Roosevelt was stricken with polio and his legs became paralyzed.

Franklin Delano Roosevelt was elected governor of New York in 1928 and president of the United States in 1932. He was re-elected president in 1936, 1940, and 1944.

Lauren Bacall, unhappy with the minor roles she was playing on Broadway, quit acting and turned to modeling.

When Lauren Bacall's picture appeared on the cover of *Harper's Bazaar* in 1943, Mrs. Howard Hawks brought the young model to the attention of her Hollywood producer-director husband. Bacall made her debut with Humphrey Bogart in *To Have and Have Not,* married him the following year, and starred in *The Big Sleep, Dark Passage,* and *Key Largo.*

David Bowie's
first solo album,
The World of David Bowie,
flopped in 1967, so he
quit the music scene, nearly
became a Buddhist monk, and
joined a mime troupe.

David Bowie became the king of glitter rock, recording such hits as
"Space Oddity," "Changes," "Suffragette City," "Young Americans,"
and "Fame," and starred in *The Elephant Man* on Broadway.

Quarterback Fran Tarkenton made 2,781 incomplete passes during his professional football career.

Fran Tarkenton holds the NFL record for most passes attempted (6,467), most passes completed (3,686), most yards passing (47,003), and most touchdown passes (342).

Gene Hackman was producer Sherwood Schwartz's first choice in 1969 to play the role of Mike Brady on *The Brady Bunch*, but Paramount executives said no.

———

Gene Hackman starred in *The French Connection* the following year and won the Academy Award for Best Actor. He also starred in *The Conversation*, *The Poseidon Adventure*, *Mississippi Burning*, *Hoosiers*, and *Unforgiven*.

John Keats' first book of poetry, published in 1817, was a financial failure.

John Keats wrote the classic poems "Ode on a Grecian Urn," "To a Nightingale," "On Melancholy," and "To Autumn."

Barbara Stanwyck dropped out of school at thirteen to wrap parcels in a Brooklyn department store.

Barbara Stanwyck became a leading lady in Hollywood movies, was nominated for four Academy Awards, and starred in *Stella Dallas*, *The Lady Eve*, *Double Indemnity*, *Meet John Doe*, and *Sorry, Wrong Number*.

Henry Clay ran for president of the United States five times but never won. He lost to John Quincy Adams, Andrew Jackson, William Henry Harrison, James Polk, and Zachary Taylor.

Henry Clay served as Secretary of State under Adams, helped form the Whig Party in 1834, and was elected to the U.S. Senate in 1849, where he sponsored the Compromise of 1850, which helped delay the Civil War for eleven years.

Van Halen's first demo tape, produced in 1976 by Kiss bassist Gene Simmons and including "Running with the Devil," was rejected by every major record company.

Van Halen signed with Warner Brothers Records the following year and their debut album, *Van Halen,* went platinum in eight months. They became the most popular American hard-rock group of the seventies, best known for their hit single "Jump."

Gene Wilder taught fencing, worked as a chauffeur, and sold toys.

Gene Wilder was nominated for an Academy Award for his role in Mel Brooks' *The Producers*. He starred in the films *Willie Wonka and the Chocolate Factory, Blazing Saddles, Young Frankenstein,* and *Stir Crazy.*

Bette Davis was fired from her first professional engagement with a stock company in Rochester, New York, by director George Cukor. In 1930, she failed a screen test at Goldwyn, and when Universal signed her later that year, studio chief Carl Laemmle said she lacked sex appeal.

Bette Davis, one of the most admired actresses of all time, won Academy Awards for *Dangerous* and *Jezebel* and starred in *Of Human Bondage, The Petrified Forest, All About Eve, What Ever Happened to Baby Jane?,* and *Hush, Hush . . . Sweet Charlotte.*

Little Richard ran off with Dr. Hudson's Medicine Show, selling snake oil at carnivals. He later washed dishes in a bus station in Macon, Georgia.

Little Richard became "the architect of rock 'n' roll" with his hit songs "Good Golly Miss Molly," "Tutti Frutti," "Long Tall Sally," and "Lucille," and starred in *Down and Out in Beverly Hills*.

Nicholas Cage, having cashed in a savings bond to rent a tuxedo and a limousine to attend the prom at Beverly Hills High School, was so nervous when his date kissed him, he threw up on his shoes. The limo driver refused to let him get back in the car, forcing Cage to walk home.

Nicholas Cage became a leading man in movies, starring in *Raising Arizona, Birdy, Moonstruck, Peggy Sue Got Married,* and *Honeymoon in Vegas.*

Leonardo da Vinci,
the illegitimate son of a lawyer,
drew detailed diagrams in his
sketchbooks showing canals
connecting the lungs to the
penis, apparently in an
inaccurate attempt to
explain erections.

Leonardo da Vinci became one of the greatest painters of the
Italian Renaissance, creating two of the most famous pictures
ever painted—the *Mona Lisa* and *The Last Supper*.

Barry Manilow worked in the CBS-TV mailroom in Manhattan and dropped out of City College of New York, where he was studying advertising.

━━━━━━━

Barry Manilow became a pop superstar as the singer and songwriter of such hits as "I Write the Songs," "Mandy," and "Copacabana."

Abbie Hoffman's
Steal This Book was rejected
by thirty publishing houses,
including Random House,
where editor Christopher Cerf,
the son of company founder
Bennett Cerf, quit his job
in protest.

Abbie Hoffman, an outspoken political activist and founder of
the Yippies, borrowed $15,000 from friends and self-published
Steal This Book. It became an instant cult classic.

Rosie O'Donnell dropped out of Boston University after her drama professor told her that the part of Rhoda Morgenstern had already been cast and she would never make it as an actress.

Rosie O'Donnell became a nationally known stand-up comedian, starred in the films *A League of Their Own* and *Harriet the Spy*, and hosts *The Rosie O'Donnell Show*.

Stephen Hawking got a 500-volt shock while trying to convert an old television set into an amplifier.

Stephen Hawking became the dominant force in the field of astrophysics and wrote the best-selling book *A Brief History of Time*.

Ronald Reagan lost the 1968 Republican nomination for president to Richard Nixon and lost the 1976 Republican nomination for president to Gerald Ford.

In 1980 at age sixty-nine, Ronald Reagan became the first divorcé and the oldest American to be elected president.

Glen Campbell dropped out of high school to join a band in Wyoming. He ended up having to sell his guitar and hitchhike home to Arizona.

Glen Campbell became a country-flavored pop recording star with a string of hugely successful hits, including "Gentle on My Mind," "Wichita Lineman," and "Galveston," and hosted the television variety show *The Glen Campbell Goodtime Hour*.

Mae West spent ten days in jail on Welfare Island for writing, directing, and starring in her first Broadway play, entitled *Sex.*

Mae West became a Hollywood sex symbol and the highest-paid woman in the United States, starring in the films *I'm No Angel, Klondike Annie,* and *My Little Chickadee.*

Jim Carrey starred on
the 1984 television sitcom
The Duck Factory (which was
canceled after three months)
and starred in the 1985 movie
Once Bitten (which bombed at
the box office).

Jim Carrey became a box-office smash as the star of the films
Dumb and Dumber, Liar Liar, The Cable Guy, The Truman Show,
and *Man on the Moon.*

Roseanne Arnold lived in a trailer and worked as a cocktail waitress.

Roseanne Arnold became the star of the number-one television sitcom *Roseanne*.

Henry Ford II, grandson of Henry Ford, was expelled from Yale University for paying a student to write a paper for him about Thomas Hardy's novels.

Henry Ford II became president of Ford Motor Company in 1945 and reorganized the company, bringing it back from the verge of bankruptcy to a profitable enterprise.

James Dean washed dishes at a tavern in New York City and lived at the YMCA. He took a job rehearsing stunts for the television game show *Beat the Clock* but was fired because contestants could not perform the stunts as easily as he could.

James Dean became the image of the restless American youth of the mid-fifties and starred in the films *East of Eden, Rebel Without a Cause,* and *Giant.*

The Who's demo record was rejected by EMI in 1965 because the group didn't write their own songs.

Pete Townshend sat down and wrote "I Can't Explain," which was released eight weeks later by Decca as the Who's first single. The Who became a major international rock act, best known for their rock operas *Tommy* and *Quadrophenia* and their hit songs "My Generation," "The Magic Bus," and "Won't Get Fooled Again."

John F. Kennedy failed to make the football team at the Canterbury School, his Connecticut prep school, and failed Latin at Choate Academy. He lost the election for president of his freshman class at Harvard University, failed to win a post on the student council as a sophomore, and dropped out of Stanford University business school.

John F. Kennedy was elected to the U.S. House of Representatives in 1946, the U.S. Senate in 1952, and the office of the 35th president of the United States in 1960.

153

Bob Newhart flunked out of law school, held several short-term jobs, then joined a Chicago accounting firm.

Bob Newhart went on to become a hugely successful stand-up comedian and the star of the sitcoms *The Bob Newhart Show* and *Newhart,* and recorded several best-selling comedy albums, most notably *The Button-Down Mind of Bob Newhart*.

Cybill Shepherd lost her bid for the title of Miss Teenage America.

Cybill Shepherd became a successful model and starred in the films *The Last Picture Show, The Heartbreak Kid,* and *Taxi Driver* and in the television series *Moonlighting*.

M. C. Hammer, unable to find work in communications or professional baseball, sold his debut single, "Ring 'Em," from the trunk of his car.

M. C. Hammer became a major rap artist, famous for his hit songs "U Can't Touch This," "Have You Seen Her," and "Pray." His album *Please Hammer Don't Hurt 'Em* sold ten million copies and remained on the charts for twenty-one weeks in 1990.

John Lindsay, after serving one term as mayor of New York City, was defeated in 1969 for renomination in the primary election of his own Republican Party.

Undaunted, John Lindsay ran for re-election as mayor of New York City in 1969 as the candidate of the Liberal and Independent parties—and won.

Henri "Papillon" Charrière, convicted in 1931 for murdering a "pimp and a stool pigeon" and sentenced to hard labor for life, made eight unsuccessful escape attempts from a penal colony in French Guiana.

Papillon was ultimately transferred to Devil's Island. He escaped in 1941, using bags of coconuts as a raft and riding the waves to Georgetown, British Guyana.

Bette Midler worked in 1965
as a go-go dancer at a bar
in Union City, New Jersey.
In 1970, she took a job as a
weekend singer at Continental Baths,
a gay Turkish bathhouse in the
basement of the Ansonia Hotel
in New York City.

At Continental Baths, Bette Midler created "the Divine Miss M," a brassy parody of a drag queen, landing her on *The Tonight Show with Johnny Carson.* She recorded albums, was nominated for an Academy Award for her role in the film *The Rose,* and starred in *Down and Out in Beverly Hills, Ruthless People,* and *Beaches.*

Ben Cohen drove an ice cream truck for Pied Piper Distributors of Hempstead, New York.

———

Ben Cohen moved to Burlington, Vermont, in 1977 and, together with his childhood friend Jerry Greenfield, opened a homemade superpremium ice cream shop. Ben & Jerry's quickly blossomed into a prominent company with such quirky flavors as Chunky Monkey, Chubby Hubby, and Cherry Garcia.

John Lennon was
frequently placed on detention
at Quarry Bank Grammar School
and received numerous canings for
"insolence," "throwing blackboard
duster out of window," "cutting class
and going AWOL," and "gambling on
school field."

John Lennon founded the Beatles, the most influential rock 'n' roll
group in history, and, as a solo artist, recorded the hit singles
"Give Peace a Chance" and "Imagine."

Thomas Alva Edison was fired from his job working in a telegraph office after one of his chemical experiments exploded.

Thomas Alva Edison became known as "the Wizard of Menlo Park" for inventing the electric light, the phonograph, and the mimeograph machine, and for improving upon the stock ticker, the telephone, the typewriter, and motion pictures.

Dustin Hoffman dropped out of Santa Monica City College and, unable to find an acting job in New York, worked as a janitor and an attendant in a hospital mental ward.

Dustin Hoffman starred in the films *The Graduate, Midnight Cowboy, Little Big Man, All the President's Men,* and *Kramer vs. Kramer.* He won an Academy Award for Best Actor in *Rain Man.*

Judd Hirsch took a three-week leave of absence from his starring role in *The Hot L Baltimore* on Broadway. While he was away, his replacement, David Groh, was "discovered" and offered the role of Rhoda Morgenstern's husband on the television sitcom *Rhoda.*

Judd Hirsch was eventually "discovered," starred in the hit television sitcoms *Taxi* and *Dear John,* and won a Tony Award for his performance in *Conversations with My Father* on Broadway.

Mariah Carey worked as a waitress, a coat-check girl, and a beauty salon janitor in New York.

Mariah Carey became an overnight sensation in 1990 with her first single "Vision of Love," won six Grammy nominations for her album *Daydream,* and recorded the hit songs "Emotions," "Dreamlover," "Honey," and "Fantasy."

Benjamin Franklin attended school
in Boston for only two years,
cut wicks and melted tallow
in his father's candle shop,
and at seventeen ran away
to Philadelphia.

━━━━━━

As a boy, Benjamin Franklin taught himself algebra, geometry, navigation, grammar, logic, French, German, Italian, Spanish, and Latin. As an adult, he founded the *Pennsylvania Gazette,* published *Poor Richard's Almanac,* proved that lightning is electricity, invented bifocal lenses, founded the University of Pennsylvania, served as minister to France, and signed the Declaration of Independence and the United States Constitution.

Bob Dylan ran away to Chicago at age ten, traveled with a Texas carnival at thirteen, and dropped out of the University of Minnesota.

Bob Dylan became the most influential songwriter in rock history, best known for his songs "Blowin' in the Wind," "The Times They Are A-Changin'," "Like a Rolling Stone," "Rainy Day Women #12 & 35," and "Mr. Tambourine Man."

Charles Schulz asked his girlfriend, Donna Johnson, to marry him, but she turned him down and married a fireman instead.

Charles Schulz created the beloved comic strip *Peanuts* and immortalized Donna Johnson as the Little Red-Haired Girl who constantly rejects Charlie Brown. *Peanuts* ran daily in 73 countries and earned Schulz $30 to $40 million annually.

Alfred Hitchcock worked as a technical estimator of electric cables for a telegraph company.

Alfred Hitchcock became internationally renowned as the master of the suspense genre. He directed more than sixty films, including *The Thirty-Nine Steps, The Lady Vanishes, Rebecca, Suspicion, Lifeboat, Spellbound, Notorious, Strangers on a Train, Rear Window, Vertigo, North by Northwest,* and *Psycho.*

James Joyce, the author of *Dubliners* and *A Portrait of the Artist as a Young Man*, lived in poverty and obscurity.

When his novel *Ulysses* was published in 1922,
James Joyce became one of the most celebrated authors
of the twentieth century.

Richard Nixon lost the race
for president of the United States
to John F. Kennedy in 1960 and,
after losing the race for California
governor to Edmund Brown
in 1962, told reporters in
his concession speech,
"You won't have Dick Nixon
to kick around anymore."

Richard Nixon was elected the 37th president of the United States
in 1968 and was re-elected by a landslide in 1972.

Errol Flynn attended several prestigious schools in Australia and England and was expelled from most of them.

Errol Flynn became a legendary Hollywood swashbuckler, starring in *The Charge of the Light Brigade*, *Captain Blood*, *The Prince and the Pauper*, and *The Adventures of Robin Hood*.

Raquel Welch worked as a cocktail waitress in Dallas, Texas, to save up enough money to have her nose fixed.

Raquel Welch became a sex goddess in the sixties and one of the highest-paid women in show business, starring in *Fantastic Voyage, One Million Years B.C.,* and *Myra Breckinridge.*

Theodore Dreiser's first novel,
Sister Carrie, was sold to Doubleday,
but when Mrs. Doubleday, the wife of
the company's president, objected to
the manuscript's immorality, the
publisher tried to cancel the book
contract. Dreiser insisted that the
contract be honored, so Doubleday
published the book in 1900 but
refused to distribute or advertise it.

Twelve years later, Theodore Dreiser got another publisher to print
Sister Carrie. Dreiser, considered the foremost American writer in
the naturalism movement, also wrote *An American Tragedy.*

John Travolta dropped out of Dwight Morrow High School in Englewood, New Jersey, at age sixteen.

John Travolta played Vinnie Barbarino on the television sitcom *Welcome Back, Kotter* and starred in the movies *Saturday Night Fever, Grease, Pulp Fiction, Get Shorty, Primary Colors,* and *A Civil Action.*

Bernard Marcus and
Arthur Blank, two executives
with Handy Dan Home
Improvement Centers,
lost their jobs in 1978
due to a corporate buyout.

Bernard Marcus and Arthur Blank teamed up with a third Handy Dan co-worker, Ronald Brill, and in 1979 the trio launched a do-it-yourself home improvement warehouse store called Home Depot, now North America's largest home improvement retailer.

Katie Couric was banned from reading news reports on the air by the president of CNN, who insisted she had an irritating, high-pitched, squeaky voice.

After working with a voice coach, Katie Couric became a television news reporter and a popular host on the *Today* show.

Steve McQueen worked as a towel boy in a brothel in the Dominican Republic, got fired from a job selling pencils in a traveling carnival, and was thrown in the brig for forty-one days for going AWOL from the Marines to visit his girlfriend. He landed his first paying role in a Yiddish theater, where he had one line ("Nothing will help" in Yiddish), but after the fourth night, he was fired.

Steve McQueen became the most popular and highest-paid screen personality of the sixties and seventies. He starred in *The Magnificent Seven, The Great Escape, Bullitt, The Getaway,* and *Papillon.*

Willie Nelson sold encyclopedias and vacuum cleaners and, frustrated by his failed attempts to make it as a musician, became a pig farmer.

Willie Nelson became a country music superstar, famous for his hit songs "To All the Girls I've Loved Before," "Always on My Mind," "Mamas, Don't Let Your Babies Grow Up to Be Cowboys," "Good Hearted Woman," and "On the Road Again." He starred in the movies *Electric Horseman* and *Wag the Dog*.

F. Scott Fitzgerald failed
algebra, history, French, and
physics during his second year
at the Newman School,
a Catholic boarding school in
Hackensack, New Jersey, and
dropped out of Princeton
University in 1917.

F. Scott Fitzgerald became a leading writer during the
Roaring Twenties. He is best known for his novels
This Side of Paradise, The Great Gatsby, and *Tender Is the Night.*

Rosa Parks, a 42-year-old seamstress, was arrested and fined $14 for refusing to give her seat to a white man on a bus in Montgomery, Alabama, in 1955.

Rosa Parks fought the segregation law in court, compelling Martin Luther King, Jr., to lead the black community to boycott city buses and prompting the Supreme Court to declare the blacks-in-back ordinance unconstitutional—paving the course for civil rights in the United States.

Al Pacino dropped out of Manhattan's High School for the Performing Arts at age seventeen and worked as a delivery boy, usher, porter, and apartment-building superintendent.

Al Pacino won two Tony Awards on Broadway and won an Academy Award for *The Scent of a Woman*. He portrayed Michael Corleone in *The Godfather* trilogy and starred in the films *Serpico, Dog Day Afternoon, Scarface,* and *Glengarry Glen Ross*.

Harry Nilsson worked the night shift as a computer specialist at the Security First National Bank in Van Nuys, California.

Harry Nilsson became a singer-songwriter, best known for his hit songs "One" (sung by Three Dog Night), "Everybody's Talkin'" (the theme song to *Midnight Cowboy*), the top ten "Coconut," and "Jump into the Fire."

Ponce de León set sail from Puerto Rico in 1513 to find the imaginary Fountain of Youth. His absurd quest failed.

Instead, Ponce de León wound up discovering the Florida and Yucatán peninsulas.

Babe Ruth was raised in a Catholic school for delinquents in Baltimore.

Babe Ruth became the first great home-run hitter in baseball history, hitting 714 home runs during his career playing for the Boston Red Sox and the New York Yankees.

Tony Curtis was a member of a notorious Bronx street gang.

Tony Curtis was nominated for an Academy Award for his role in *The Defiant Ones* and starred in the films *Houdini, Some Like It Hot, Spartacus, The List of Adrian Messenger,* and *The Great Race.*

Fred Schneider worked
in a vegetarian restaurant,
Keith Strickland and Ricky Wilson
worked at local bus stations,
and Cindy Wilson made shakes at
the Kress's Whirli-Q luncheonette
in Athens, Georgia.

Schneider, Strickland, the Wilsons, and Kate Pierson formed the B-52's, a wildly successful party band, with such hits as "Rock Lobster," "Planet Claire," "Private Idaho," and "Love Shack."

Charles Dickens dropped out of school at age fourteen.

Charles Dickens became one of the most popular writers of all time. His best-known novels include *A Christmas Carol, David Copperfield, Great Expectations, Oliver Twist,* and *A Tale of Two Cities.*

Elliott Gould worked as an elevator operator in a hotel.

Elliott Gould starred in the films *The Night They Raided Minsky's, Bob & Carol & Ted & Alice, M*A*S*H,* and *The Long Goodbye.*

Ruth Bader Ginsburg
ran for student government at
James Madison High School
in Brooklyn, New York—and lost.
In 1959, after her graduation from
the Columbia Law School
(tied for first place in her class),
not one major law firm in
New York City offered her a job
—because she was a woman.

Ruth Bader Ginsburg was appointed to the U.S. Supreme Court in 1993 by President Bill Clinton, making her the second female justice in the Court's history.

Davy Jones
was an apprentice jockey at
Newmarket Racetrack in England.
After playing the Artful Dodger in
Oliver! on Broadway and being put
under contract with Columbia Pictures,
he seriously considered a
return to jockeying.

▬▬▬▬▬▬▬

Davy Jones was soon chosen to star in the television show *The Monkees,* became a teen idol, and sang the hit songs "A Little Bit Me, A Little Bit You," "Daydream Believer," and "Valleri."

Mick Jagger, the lead singer of the rock group Blues Incorporated, was deemed "unsuitable" by the BBC to sing on the radio program "Jazz Club" in 1962.

Mick Jagger became the lead singer of the Rolling Stones, "the greatest rock 'n' roll band in the world," famous for their hit songs "Satisfaction," "Jumpin' Jack Flash," "Honky Tonk Woman," "Brown Sugar," and "Start Me Up."

Sinead O'Connor was placed in a residential center run by Dominican nuns for girls with behavior problems after she was caught shoplifting. She later worked part-time in Dublin as a Kiss-o-gram French maid.

Sinead O'Connor became a singer-songwriter best known for her album *I Do Not Want What I Haven't Got,* recorded the hit song "Nothing Compares 2 U," and achieved infamy for tearing a picture of the Pope in half on *Saturday Night Live*.

Harrison Ford failed philosophy in his senior year at Ripon College in Wisconsin and never received his degree. Following a forty-five-second role in his first movie, *Dead Heat on a Merry-Go-Round,* a Columbia executive told him, "You ain't got it, kid!" After bit roles in *Gunsmoke* and *The Virginian,* Ford quit acting for a while and became a carpenter.

Harrison Ford became a Hollywood superstar, starring as Han Solo in the *Star Wars* movies and as Indiana Jones in the *Raiders of the Lost Ark* movies. He also starred in the films *Blade Runner, Witness, Patriot Games, The Fugitive,* and *Airforce One.*

Conan O'Brien created a pilot for a television series called *Lookwell*, starring Adam West, which never sold to any network.

———

Conan O'Brien went on to become host of the television talk show *Late Night with Conan O'Brien*.

John Amos
was a running back
for the Denver Broncos
for twenty-four hours before
being cut from the team.
He was later dropped by another
twelve professional football teams,
including the Kansas City Chiefs.

John Amos went on to star as Gordy the Weatherman on
The Mary Tyler Moore Show, James Evans on *Good Times*, and
the adult Kunta Kinte in *Roots*, the most-watched program
in television history.

Randy Bachman and
C. F. Turner left the Guess Who,
the most popular rock 'n' roll
band in Canada, and formed
Bachman-Turner Overdrive,
whose initial demo record
was rejected by twenty-four
record companies.

Bachman-Turner Overdrive eventually signed with Mercury
Records and released the hit singles "You Ain't Seen Nothin' Yet"
and "Taking Care of Business."

Malcolm X was sentenced to jail for burglary in Massachusetts at age twenty.

Malcolm X became a leading spokesman for Black Muslims and formed the Organization of Afro-American Unity to unite black people throughout the world.

F. W. Woolworth, convinced
that a store that sold only
merchandise priced less than
five cents would be an instant success,
opened the Great Five Cent Store
in Utica, New York, in 1879.
The store failed.

Undaunted, F. W. Woolworth moved to Lancaster, Pennsylvania,
in the heart of the Amish country, and opened the world's first
five-and-dime store at 21 North Queens Street. This time,
the store succeeded, launching the Woolworth empire.

Dean Martin flopped as a boxer, worked in a steel mill, and dealt poker in a gambling den.

Dean Martin teamed with Jerry Lewis to become one of the most phenomenal successes in show-business history. He starred in dozens of movies (including *My Friend Irma*, the Matt Helm movies, and *Airport*), became a member of the famous Rat Pack, and hosted a television variety series, *The Dean Martin Show*.

John Adams lost the election against George Washington for first president of the United States.

John Adams became the first vice president of the United States and the country's second president.

Madonna worked in a doughnut shop in Times Square.

Madonna became an international celebrity and one of the highest-paid female entertainers of all time. Her hit songs include "Borderline," "Like a Virgin," "Material Girl," "Papa Don't Preach," and "Open Your Heart," and she starred in the movies *Desperately Seeking Susan, A League of Their Own,* and *Evita*.

Fred Smith, a student at
Yale University in the 1960s,
received a "C" on a
term paper outlining his
business plan for a
reliable overnight
delivery service.

Undaunted, Fred Smith raised $40 million from investors, $8 million from his family, and $90 million in bank loans to launch Federal Express in 1973. Today, as FedEx Chairman, President, and Chief Executive Officer, Fred Smith earns an annual salary of more than $1.2 million.

Albert Einstein worked as an examiner at the Swiss Patent Office in Bern.

Albert Einstein became one of the greatest scientists of all time, contributing to the quantum theory, developing the theory of relativity, and confirming the atomic theory of matter.

Boris Yeltsin was expelled from elementary school for a speech he made at the graduation ceremony —accusing a teacher of subjecting students to "cruel, unusual punishment" and then demanding her dismissal.

Boris Yeltsin was elected president of the Russian Federation in 1991, led protesters to defeat an attempted coup against general secretary Mikhail Gorbachev, and, after the Soviet Union was disbanded in 1991, became head of the Commonwealth of Independent States.

James Taylor committed himself in 1963 to the McLean psychiatric hospital in Belmont, Massachusetts, and in 1968 entered the Austin Riggs Hospital in Stockbridge, Massachusetts, to kick heroin addiction.

James Taylor became a rock superstar with his 1970 album *Sweet Baby James* and recorded the hit songs "Fire and Rain," "You've Got a Friend," "How Sweet It Is (To Be Loved by You)," and "Handy Man."

Burt Lancaster dropped out of New York University, toured as a circus acrobat, and later worked as a refrigerator repairman.

Burt Lancaster won an Academy Award for his role in *Elmer Gantry*. He starred in the films *The Killers, From Here to Eternity, Gunfight at the O.K. Corral, Bird Man of Alcatraz,* and *Atlantic City*.

James Brown dropped out
of the seventh grade,
was sentenced to hard labor
at a Georgia state
correctional institute at
sixteen for petty theft,
and served four years at
the Alto Reform School
in Georgia.

James Brown became "the godfather of soul," best known for
the hit songs "Papa's Got a Brand New Bag" and
"I Got You (I Feel Good)."

Jerry Lewis had to repeat the fifth grade and was expelled from high school in Irvington, New Jersey, for punching the principal in the mouth and knocking out one of his teeth. The principal had called Lewis a "dumb Jew" for causing an explosion in the chemistry lab.

Jerry Lewis teamed up with Dean Martin and the two became the most popular comedy team in America in the 1940s, starring in more than sixteen movies together. His dozens of solo films include *The Geisha Boy, The Bellboy, The Nutty Professor, Who's Minding the Store?,* and *The King of Comedy.* He also hosts an annual Labor Day telethon for muscular dystrophy.

Louis Armstrong was found guilty of juvenile delinquency and sentenced to live in the Home for Colored Waifs in New Orleans.

While living in the children's home, Louis Armstrong learned to play the cornet and later became the first internationally famous jazz soloist and the first jazz musician to sing in the scat style of rhythmic nonsense syllables. He is best known for his hit records "Hello, Dolly" and "Mack the Knife."

Clark Gable
stood on street corners
dressed as a clown to hawk customers
for a traveling tent show,
worked as a lumberjack,
and sold neckties at
Meir and Frank's department store
in Portland, Oregon.

———

Clark Gable became known as the king of Hollywood, starred as Rhett Butler in *Gone With the Wind,* and won an Academy Award for his role in *It Happened One Night.* He appeared in more than seventy films, most notably *Red Dust, Mutiny on the Bounty, San Francisco, The Hucksters,* and *The Misfits.*

Lily Tomlin dropped out as a pre-med student from Wayne State University in Detroit, Michigan.

Lily Tomlin became famous as telephone operator Ernestine and five-year-old Edith Ann on *Rowan & Martin's Laugh-In*, starred in one-woman shows on Broadway, released several hit comedy albums, and appeared in the films *Nashville* and *9 to 5*.

Steven Spielberg's mediocre grades prevented him from getting into UCLA film school. Instead, he majored in English at California State University in Long Beach but dropped out during his junior year.

Steven Spielberg went on to produce four of the top ten films of all time (*Jaws, E.T., Indiana Jones and the Last Crusade,* and *Jurassic Park*), co-founded DreamWorks, and won Academy Awards for directing *Schindler's List* and *Saving Private Ryan*.

The Ramones played their first gig in August 1974 at the New York club CBGB before an audience of five people and a dog.

The Ramones invented punk rock, landed a recording contract with Sire Records, and released the hit songs "Rockaway Beach," "Sheena Is a Punk Rocker," and "I Wanna Be Sedated."

Ray Bolger worked as a bank clerk, a vacuum cleaner salesman, and an accountant.

Ray Bolger went on to achieve worldwide fame as the Scarecrow in *The Wizard of Oz*.

Betty Friedan was fired from her job as a reporter in 1952 for requesting maternity leave, and a man was hired to replace her.

Her experience as a housewife prompted Betty Friedan to write a book, *The Feminine Mystique,* published in 1963, which became a best-seller and helped ignite the feminist movement in America.

Ray Kroc dropped out of high school and worked as a jazz pianist, a paper-cup salesman, and a milk-shake-machine distributor.

Ray Kroc negotiated franchise rights for a hamburger joint in San Bernardino, California, run by the McDonald brothers, and launched the McDonald's fast-food empire.

Peter Tork flunked out of Carleton College, spent fourteen months working at a Connecticut thread factory, and returned to Carleton only to flunk out again.

Peter Tork went on to star in the television series *The Monkees* and wrote the show's closing theme song, "For Pete's Sake."

Ray Davies dropped out of
William Grimshaw Secondary School
in London, and his brother
Dave Davies was expelled
after being caught in a
compromising position
with a girl.

The Davies brothers founded the Kinks, one of the most influential rock 'n' roll groups of the sixties, best known for their hit songs "You Really Got Me," "All Day and All of the Night," "Lola," "Sunny Afternoon," and "A Rock 'n' Roll Fantasy."

George W. Bush pleaded guilty in 1976 to drunk driving in Maine.

George W. Bush was elected governor of Texas in 1994, re-elected in 1998, and elected 43rd president of the United States in 2000.

President Grover Cleveland lost his bid for re-election in 1884 to Benjamin Harrison.

Grover Cleveland ran against Harrison four years later and won a second term, becoming the only president in U.S. history to serve two nonconsecutive terms.

Rip Torn hitchhiked from Texas to Hollywood in hopes of immediate stardom, only to become a short-order cook and a dishwasher.

Rip Torn starred as Artie on the television comedy series
The Larry Sanders Show and appeared in the movies
The Seduction of Joe Tynan, Betrayal, and *Defending Your Life*.

Brian Epstein was expelled
from Liverpool College,
was discharged from the
Royal Army Service Corps
after four psychiatrists concluded
that he was unfit for military service,
and dropped out of the
Royal Academy of Dramatic Arts.

Brian Epstein became a highly successful manager in the
music industry, managing the Beatles, Gerry and the Pacemakers,
Billy J. Kramer and the Dakotas, and Cilla Black.

Marlene Dietrich
was fired as a violinist
with a German orchestra
accompanying silent films
because her legs were
too much of a
distraction to the other
members of the orchestra.

Marlene Dietrich became a glamorous and sensuous Hollywood starlet, appearing in *The Blue Angel, Shanghai Express, The Scarlet Express, A Foreign Affair,* and *Touch of Evil.*

John Cheever
was expelled from
Thayer Academy,
a prestigious Massachusetts
prep school, in 1930,
after failing French,
Latin, and math.

John Cheever went on to write a short story about the experience, titled it "Expelled," and sold it to the *New Republic,* which published it that same year. He became a regular contributor to *The New Yorker* and won the Pulitzer Prize for his last collection of short stories.

Danny DeVito, trained at the Wilfred Academy of Hair and Beauty Culture, worked at age eighteen as a hairdresser at his sister's beauty salon.

Danny DeVito went on to win an Emmy Award as Louie De Palma on the hit sitcom *Taxi* and starred in the movies *Romancing the Stone, Throw Mama from the Train, Tin Men, The War of the Roses,* and *Renaissance Man.*

Clarence Earl Gideon, having served time for four previous felonies, was sentenced in 1961 to serve five years in prison for breaking into the Bay Harbor Poolroom in Panama City, Florida.

———

Clarence Earl Gideon, insisting that he had been denied due process of law because the court had refused his request for a lawyer, convinced the Supreme Court to rule that the Sixth Amendment guarantees legal counsel in state criminal trials —a ruling that revolutionized the American justice system. Gideon was provided with a lawyer, retried, and acquitted.

Barry White served three months in jail in 1960 for stealing three hundred tires from a Los Angeles car dealer.

Barry White became the romantic booming baritone voice of soul with his hit songs "Can't Get Enough of Your Love, Babe" and "You're the First, the Last, My Everything."

227

Mahatma Gandhi, having studied law in London, returned to India in 1891 to practice law but met with little success and moved to South Africa.

Mahatma Gandhi went on to free India from British control through nonviolent resistance and became known as the father of India.

Elton John struggled as a member of several unsuccessful rock groups in the 1960s, and his first single, "Come Back, Baby," released with his band Bluesology, never made the charts. He failed an audition for Liberty Records, and his 1968 debut album, *Empty Skies*, flopped.

Elton John became the single most successful pop artist of the seventies, best known for his albums *Madman Across the Water*, *Goodbye Yellow Brick Road*, and *Captain Fantastic & The Brown Dirt Cowboy*. His hit songs include "Daniel," "Rocket Man," "Candle in the Wind," "Don't Let the Sun Go Down on Me," and "I Guess That's Why They Call It the Blues."

J. Robert Oppenheimer was stripped naked at summer camp, beaten up, painted green, and then locked in the icehouse overnight.

J. Robert Oppenheimer became a physicist, a member of the Manhattan Project at Los Alamos, New Mexico, and earned the title "father of the atomic bomb."

Jerry Lee Lewis was expelled from Assembly of God Institute Bible School in Waxahachie, Texas.

Jerry Lee Lewis became a rock 'n' roll legend with his hits "Great Balls of Fire" and "Whole Lotta Shakin' Goin' On."

Garry Marshall applied to the *New York Times* for a job as a copyboy, but "they told me they only like Ivy League graduates. I insisted I could get coffee just as fast as any Harvard kid, but they didn't buy it."

Garry Marshall created the sitcoms *The Odd Couple, Happy Days, Laverne & Shirley,* and *Mork & Mindy,* directed the films *The Flamingo Kid, Nothing in Common, Beaches, Pretty Woman,* and *Dear God,* and played Stan Lansing on *Murphy Brown.*

Janis Joplin hitchhiked from Austin, Texas, to San Francisco in 1963 to pursue a singing career but, getting no further than a few sporadic singing jobs, returned to Texas.

Janis Joplin became one of the greatest blues singers of all time with such hit songs as "Piece of My Heart," "Down on Me," "Try (Just a Little Bit Harder)," and "Me and Bobby McGee" and a riveting performance at Woodstock in 1969.

Donald Fisher, a real estate developer, found it impossible in 1969 to exchange a pair of Levi's jeans for a different size at a department store in San Francisco.

Frustrated by the experience, Donald Fisher opened his own store specializing in jeans and called it The Gap, which became one of the most successful specialty chains in retailing history.

Dick Van Dyke ran a small advertising agency that quickly went out of business.

Dick Van Dyke went on to win an Emmy Award three years in a row as the star of television's *The Dick Van Dyke Show*. He also starred in the movies *Bye Bye Birdie, Mary Poppins,* and *Chitty Chitty Bang Bang*.

Moses killed an Egyptian taskmaster and fled the country, according to the biblical book of Exodus.

Moses led the exodus of the Hebrew slaves from Egypt, received the Ten Commandments at Mount Sinai, and led the Hebrew people to the Promised Land.

Sarah Bernhardt was suspended three times from convent school for unruly behavior. When critics panned her stage debut in 1862, the seventeen-year-old Bernhardt tried to poison herself by drinking liquid rouge and was fired after a fight with a respected actress in the cast.

Sarah Bernhardt became the world's first theatrical superstar, admired for the grace and poetry of her stage movement and best known for her performance in *Camille*.

237

Lyndon Johnson was kicked out of
Southwest Texas State Teachers College,
drove to California in a
1918 Model T Ford with four friends
(without telling his parents), and
worked as an elevator operator,
grape picker, dishwasher, law clerk,
and auto mechanic.

███████

Lyndon Johnson was elected to the U.S. House of Representatives
in 1937, the U.S. Senate in 1948, and became Senate majority
leader in 1955. He was elected vice president of the United States
on the ticket with John F. Kennedy in 1960,
became president upon Kennedy's assassination in 1963,
and was elected for a full term in 1964.

Boy George was expelled from Eltham Green High School in Kent, England.

Boy George became lead singer of Culture Club and had six top ten hits, including "Do You Really Want to Hurt Me," "Karma Chameleon," and "The Crying Game."

Paul Orfalea, a dyslexic who failed second grade, was erroneously put in a school for the mentally retarded for six weeks.

Paul Orfalea, nicknamed Kinko after his red Afro haircut, went on to found Kinko's, the most successful photocopy chain in the United States.

The Sex Pistols' first single,
"Anarchy in the U.K.,"
caused the band to be dropped
by their record label, EMI,
and their second single,
"God Save the Queen
(She Ain't a Human Being),"
was banned by the BBC.

―――――

The Sex Pistols forged the identity of punk rock in the seventies
with their debut album, *Never Mind the Bollocks*.

Joe Louis delivered ice, worked in an automobile factory, and studied carpentry.

Joe Louis went on to become the world heavyweight boxing champion in 1937, holding the title longer than any other man, defending his title twenty-five times, and scoring twenty knockouts.

John Grisham's first novel, *A Time to Kill,* was rejected by sixteen agents and a dozen publishing houses. Wynwood Press published 5,000 copies of *A Time to Kill* in 1989, but sales were dismal.

John Grisham became the best-selling author of *The Firm* and *The Pelican Brief,* prompting Dell to publish *A Time to Kill* in paperback in 1992. It was made into a motion picture in 1996.

Gene Kelly worked as a dance instructor, a ditch digger, and a gas station attendant.

Gene Kelly revolutionized Hollywood musicals with his imaginative dance routines. He starred in *Pal Joey* on Broadway and in the movies *For Me and My Gal, Ziegfeld Follies, An American in Paris, Singin' in the Rain,* and *Inherit the Wind.*

Bill Cosby dropped out of high school and worked in a shoe repair shop and a car muffler plant.

Bill Cosby became a hugely successful stand-up comedian and the first black to star in a dramatic television series (as Alexander Scott in *I Spy*). He later starred in the hit family sitcom *The Cosby Show* and became the commercial spokesperson for Jell-O brand pudding.

Audie Murphy dropped out of school when he was fourteen and worked as a farmhand, cotton picker, grocery store clerk, and gas station attendant.

Audie Murphy became the most decorated United States soldier of World War II, receiving twenty-four medals, including the Medal of Honor. He played himself in the movie *To Hell and Back* and also starred in *The Red Badge of Courage, Destry,* and *The Quiet American.*

William Penn, expelled from
Oxford for opposing the
university's rule that everyone
must attend the Church of England,
was imprisoned three times
for writing and preaching
about the Quaker faith.

William Penn ultimately persuaded King Charles II to allow the
Quakers to set up a colony in America and, after securing the
promise of religious freedom, founded Pennsylvania.

Thomas Monaghan, having grown up in an orphanage and several foster homes, dropped out of a Catholic seminary, served in the marines, and then dropped out of college.

Thomas Monaghan borrowed $900 in 1960 and bought a failed pizza parlor in Ypsilanti, Michigan, with his brother James. A year later, Monaghan traded a Volkswagen Beetle for his brother's half of the company. That company became Domino's Pizza, the world leader in pizza delivery, with more than 5,200 restaurants.

Buddy Ebsen, cast to play the role of the Tin Man in *The Wizard of Oz*, suffered an allergic reaction to the aluminum dust used to powder his face and was replaced two weeks into shooting by Jack Haley.

Buddy Ebsen later struck it rich starring as Jed Clampett in the long-running television comedy series *The Beverly Hillbillies* and again as the star of the popular detective series *Barnaby Jones*.

Mary Leakey was expelled from a convent school in England for refusing to recite poetry. She was expelled from a second convent school for deliberately setting off an explosion in chemistry class.

Mary Leakey became a world-renowned anthropologist, found a human-like skull approximately 1.75 million years old in Tanzania's Olduvai Gorge, and together with her husband, Louis Leakey, found fragments of a human-like jaw and teeth about 14 million years old in Kenya.

Boris Karloff, unable to support himself as an actor, worked as a truck driver.

Boris Karloff became the king of horror films, starring in more than one hundred movies, including *Frankenstein, The Mummy, The Bride of Frankenstein, The Raven,* and *Son of Frankenstein.*

William Thackeray dropped out of Cambridge University in his second year and gambled away his inheritance.

William Thackeray, one of the great novelists of the English Victorian age, wrote *Vanity Fair*.

James Garner dropped out of the University of Oklahoma and worked as a traveling salesman, carpet layer, and swimsuit model.

James Garner starred in the television series *Maverick* and *The Rockford Files*.

Bo Diddley performed on street corners.

Bo Diddley became one of the most influential, innovative, and original R&B musicians the world has ever seen.

Michael Caine dropped out of school at age fifteen and served tea in a London theater.

Michael Caine starred in *Alfie*, *Sleuth*, and won Academy Awards as Best Supporting Actor for *Hannah and Her Sisters* and *The Cider House Rules*.

Thomas Jefferson lost the election for president of the United States in 1796 to John Adams.

Four years later, Thomas Jefferson beat John Adams to be elected third president of the United States.

Sam Walton, the owner of fifteen
Ben Franklin self-service hardware store
franchises running under
the name Walton's Five & Dime,
proposed opening discount stores
in small towns in 1962,
but Ben Franklin executives
rejected the idea.

Undaunted, Sam Walton and his brother Bud opened the first
Wal-Mart Discount City in Rogers, Arkansas, in 1962, founding a
discount store empire.

Rick James went AWOL from the U.S. Navy in 1965 and moved to Toronto, Canada.

Rick James became a successful funk musician, best known for his disco hits "Super Freak" and "Give It to Me Baby."

Miguel de Cervantes, wounded at the battle of Lepanto in 1571, lost the use of his left hand, was captured by pirates in 1575, and spent the next five years as a prisoner at Algiers.

Miguel de Cervantes became the author of *Don Quixote*.

Neil Diamond, a pre-med major on a fencing scholarship, dropped out of New York University six months before graduation.

———

Neil Diamond became a pop singer and songwriter, penning the hit songs "I'm a Believer," "Sweet Caroline," "Song Sung Blue," "America," and "Heartlight."

James Madison, having served one year in the Virginia legislative assembly, lost his bid for re-election in 1797.

James Madison was elected fourth president of the United States in 1808 and was re-elected in 1812.

Otis Redding dropped out of Ballard-Hudson Senior High School in Dawson, Georgia, moved to Los Angeles to break into music, ended up working at a car wash for six months, and returned to Georgia.

Otis Redding became a legendary soul singer, best known for his hit song "(Sittin' On) The Dock of the Bay."

Richard Pryor was expelled from high school for punching out a science teacher.

Richard Pryor became one of America's most popular comedians and starred in *Silver Streak, Lady Sings the Blues, Stir Crazy, Brewster's Millions,* and several concert films.

Debbie Gibson, offered the lead role in the Broadway production of *Les Misérables* in 1985, was dropped when the producers discovered she was only fifteen.

Debbie Gibson signed a contract with Atlantic Records the next year and became a pop phenomenon as a singer-songwriter with five top ten singles: "Only in My Dreams," "Shake Your Love," "Out of the Blue," "Foolish Beat," and "Lost in Your Eyes."

Lee J. Cobb ran away from
home in New York City
at age seventeen and went to
Hollywood in hopes of making
a career in films, but failed.
He returned home, where he
studied accounting at
City College of New York.

Lee J. Cobb created the role of Willy Loman on Broadway in
Arthur Miller's *Death of a Salesman* and starred in the television
series *The Virginian* and dozens of movies, including
On the Waterfront, The Three Faces of Eve, and *The Exorcist.*

Pablo Picasso, a poor student in elementary school, was often punished by being sent to the "cell," a room where he sat on a bench, isolated from the other students.

Pablo Picasso used his time in solitary isolation to "take a pad of paper and draw nonstop" and became the most famous and innovative painter of the twentieth century, developing cubism.

Frank Capra, unable to find work as a chemical engineer, sold books and mining stocks door to door and played poker for a living.

Frank Capra won three Academy Awards for Best Director.
His films include *It Happened One Night, Mr. Deeds Goes to Town, You Can't Take It with You, Meet John Doe,* and *It's a Wonderful Life.*

Rudolph Valentino worked as a gigolo and petty thief.

Rudolph Valentino became the most popular romantic idol of silent movies, starring as a desert warrior in *The Sheik* and *Son of the Sheik.*

Joan Crawford worked as a laundress, waitress, and shopgirl.

Joan Crawford became one of Hollywood's great sex symbols, winning an Academy Award for her role in *Mildred Pierce* and starring in such classics as *Grand Hotel, Flamingo Road,* and *What Ever Happened to Baby Jane?*

Cleopatra was ousted as the Queen of Egypt in 48 B.C.E. by her brother Ptolemy's guardians.

Later that year, Cleopatra persuaded Julius Caesar to defeat her opponents and restore her to the Egyptian throne. In 34 B.C.E., Cleopatra convinced Mark Anthony to appoint her ruler of Egypt, Cyprus, Crete, and Syria.

Warren Beatty washed dishes for a living, carted sand for builders of the third tube of the Lincoln Tunnel, and played piano in a cocktail lounge.

Warren Beatty became a Hollywood sex symbol, starring in *Splendor in the Grass*, *Bonnie and Clyde*, *Heaven Can Wait*, *Reds,* and *Bulworth*.

James Thurber submitted several stories to *The New Yorker* in 1926, but all of them were rejected. He then wrote a 30,000-word story called *Why We Behave Like Microbe Hunters,* which was rejected by numerous magazines and book publishers.

James Thurber became known as a comic genius for his short stories and cartoons in *The New Yorker*, most notably "The Secret Life of Walter Mitty," and for his books *The Thurber Carnival, Is Sex Necessary?* (written with E. B. White), and *My Life and Hard Times*.

Irving Berlin worked as a singing waiter.

Irving Berlin went on to compose more than one thousand songs, including "Alexander's Rag Time Band," "Easter Parade," "Cheek to Cheek," "There's No Business Like Show Business," and "Anything You Can Do." He wrote the Broadway musicals *Annie Get Your Gun* and *This Is the Army,* received the Congressional Gold Medal for his song "God Bless America," and won an Academy Award for his song "White Christmas."

Abraham Lincoln, after gaining national attention in the Lincoln-Douglas debates, lost the 1858 race for Senator from Illinois to incumbent Stephen Douglas.

Two years later, Abraham Lincoln was elected 16th president of the United States.

Elvis Costello dropped out of high school at age sixteen and, in 1973, became a computer operator at an Elizabeth Arden cosmetics factory in London.

Elvis Costello went on to become an innovative singer-songwriter
with his hit albums *This Year's Model, My Aim Is True,
Get Happy!!,* and *Imperial Bedroom* and the hit songs "Alison"
and "Watching the Detectives."

Vladimir Lenin was expelled from
law school at Kazan University
after just three months in 1887
for participating in a student
demonstration protesting the lack of
student freedom in the school.
He applied several times to re-enter
the university—unsuccessfully.

Vladimir Lenin founded the Communist Party in Russia, led the
Russian revolution, and became the world's first Communist
dictator, establishing the Soviet Union.

George Burns worked for a ladies' blouse manufacturer.

George Burns teamed up with Gracie Allen to form one of the most popular comedy teams in show business, starred in *The George Burns and Gracie Allen Show* on radio and television, won an Academy Award for his role in *The Sunshine Boys,* played God in three movies, and lived to be 100.

Kevin Costner worked as a
tour guide on sightseeing buses
of the stars' homes in Beverly Hills.
He went jobless for six months
and slept in the back of a truck.
His first films, *Sizzle Beach, U.S.A.*
and *Shadows Run Black*,
were soft-core porn flicks.

━━━━━

Kevin Costner won an Academy Award for *Dances with Wolves*
and became a Hollywood heartthrob as the star of the films
Bull Durham, Field of Dreams, No Way Out, and *The Bodyguard.*

Hillary Rodham Clinton
was internationally humiliated
when her husband,
President Bill Clinton,
admitted to having had
an inappropriate relationship
with a twenty-three-year-old
White House intern.

In 2000, Hillary Rodham Clinton ran for Senator from New York
and became the first First Lady ever elected to the U.S. Senate.

Bibliography

■ *The Abbott and Costello Story* by Stephen Cox and John Lofflin (Nashville, Tennessee: Cumberland House, 1990).

■ *Adventures in the Screen Trade* by William Goldman (New York: Warner, 1984).

■ *All About the Spice Girls* (New York: Aladdin, 1997).

■ "Astronaut Charles Conrad Embodied NASA's 'Can-Do Spirit'" by Elaine Woo, *Los Angeles Times,* July 10, 1999, p. A18.

■ *Bill Cosby Superstar* by Patricia Stone Martin (Vero Beach, Florida: Rourke, 1987).

■ *Bogart: A Life in Hollywood* by Jeffrey Meyers (Boston: Houghton Mifflin, 1997).

■ *The Book of Lists* by David Wallechinsky, Irving Wallace, and Amy Wallace (New York: Bantam, 1977).

■ *Bradymania* by Elizabeth Moran (Holbrook, Massachusetts: Bob Adams, 1992).

■ "A Brief History of The Gap, Inc." (San Francisco: The Gap, Inc., 1994).

■ *Clark Gable: Portrait of a Misfit* by Jane Ellen Wayne (New York: St. Martin's, 1993).

■ *Clint Eastwood Riding High* by Douglas Thompson (Chicago: Contemporary, 1992).

■ *The Complete Directory to Prime Time Network TV Shows: 1946-Present* (Fourth Edition) by Tim Brooks and Earle Marsh (New York: Ballantine, 1992).

■ *Cruise: The Unauthorized Biography* by Frank Sanello (Dallas, Texas: Taylor, 1995).

- *Dr. Seuss & Mr. Geisel* by Judith & Neil Morgan (New York: Random House, 1995).
- *Encyclopedia of Rock Stars* by Dafydd Rees and Luke Crampton (New York: DK, 1996).
- *Encyclopedia of Sports in the United States* by Kevin Osborn (New York: Scholastic, 1997).
- *The Film Encyclopedia* by Ephraim Katz (New York: Perigee, 1979).
- "First Woman Named to Lead Blue-Chip Firm" by Joseph Menn, *Los Angeles Times,* July 20, 1999, p. A1.
- *Frank Sinatra: An American Legend* by Nancy Sinatra (Los Angeles: General, 1995).
- *George Burns and the Hundred Year Dash* by Martin Gottfried (New York: Simon & Shuster, 1996).
- *Ginger Spice in My Pocket* (New York: Smithmark, 1997).
- *The Girl with the Million Dollar Legs* by Tom McGee (Vestal, New York: The Vestal Press, 1995).
- "Giving 'Laverne And Shirley' The Funny Business" by Kirk Honeycutt, *New York Times,* April 2, 1978.
- *Great Jewish Women* by Elinor Slater & Robert Slater (Middle Village, New York: Jonathan David, 1994).
- *The Great One: The Life and Legend of Jackie Gleason* by William A. Henry III (New York: Doubleday, 1992).
- *Harrison Ford Imperfect Hero* by Garry Jenkins (Secaucus, New Jersey: Carol, 1998).
- *Her Name Is Barbra* by Randall Riese (New York: Birch Lane/Carol, 1993).
- *Hi Bob!A Self-Help Guide to the Bob Newhart Show* by Joey Green (New York: St. Martin's, 1996).
- *Hoover's Handbook of American Business 1995* (Austin, Texas: Reference, 1995).

- *The James Dean Story* by Ronald Martinetti (New York: Carol, 1975).
- "John Amos," *Denver Post,* May 18, 1977.
- *Kevin Costner: Prince of Hollywood* (London: Plexus, 1992).
- *Leading with My Chin* by Jay Leno (New York: HarperCollins, 1996).
- *The Life of Bette Davis* by Charles Higham (New York: Macmillan, 1981).
- "A Lousy Day for Golf" by Sina Moukheiber, *Forbes,* May 9, 1994.
- *Made in America* by Sam Walton with John Huey (New York: Doubleday, 1992).
- *The Making of the Wizard of Oz* by Aljean Harmetz (New York: Hyperion, 1998).
- *Marilyn Monroe* by Barbara Leaming (New York: Crown, 1998).
- *Marlene Dietrich: Life and Legend* by Steven Bach (New York: Morrow, 1992).
- *The Most Intriguing People of the Century* (New York: People Books, 1997).
- *The Official Dick Van Dyke Show Book* by Vince Waldron (New York: Hyperion, 1994).
- *The 100 Most Influential Women of All Time* by Deborah G. Felder (New York: Citadel, 1996).
- *The Oxford Companion to English Literature, Fourth Edition,* edited by Sir Paul Harvey (Oxford, England: Clarendon, 1967).
- *The Oxford Companion to Popular Music* by Peter Gammond (Oxford, England: Oxford University, 1991).
- *Pizza Tiger* by Thomas S. Monaghan with Robert Anderson (New York: Random House, 1986).
- *Rat Pack Confidential* by Shawn Levy (New York: Doubleday, 1998).
- *Remember Laughter: A Life of James Thurber* by Neil A. Graver (Lincoln, Nebraska: University of Nebraska Press, 1994).
- *Rosie O'Donnell: Her True Story* by George Mair and Anna Green (Secaucus, New Jersey: Carol, 1997).

- *The Seventies: From Hot Pants to Hot Tubs* by Andrew J. Edelstein and Kevin McDonough (New York: Dutton, 1990).
- *Shout! The Beatles in Their Generation* by Philip Norman (New York: Warner, 1981).
- *Songs My Mother Taught Me* by Marlon Brando with Robert Lindsey (Toronto: Random House, 1994).
- *Soon to Be a Major Motion Picture* by Abbie Hoffman (New York: Perigee, 1980).
- *Steve McQueen: Portrait of an American Rebel* by Marshall Terill (New York: Donald I. Fine, 1993).
- *Steven Spielberg Close Up* by George Perry (New York: Thunder Mouth, 1998).
- *Streisand: Her Life* by James Spada (New York: Crown, 1995).
- *Sunday Night at Seven* by Jack Benny and Joan Benny (New York: Warner, 1990).
- *Time Almanac Reference Edition 1994* (Washington, D.C.: Compact, 1994).
- *A Time to Kill* by John Grisham (New York: Dell, 1992).
- *The TV Encyclopedia* by David Inman (New York: Perigee, 1991).
- "Two Doughnuts and a Martini, Please" by Kerry Hannon, *Forbes,* March 9, 1987.
- *Wake Me When It's Funny* by Garry Marshall with Lori Marshall (Holbrook, Massachusetts: Adams, 1995).
- *Warren Beatty: The Last Great Lover of Hollywood* by John Parker (New York: Carol & Graf, 1993).
- *When They Were Kids* by Carol Orsag Madigan and Ann Elwood (New York: Random House, 1998).
- *The World Almanac and Book of Facts 1996* (New York: Scripps Howard, 1996).
- *The World Book Encyclopedia* (Chicago: World Book, 1985).
- *World Religions: From Ancient History to the Present,* edited by Geoffrey Parrinder (New York: Facts on File, 1985).

Index

Adams, John, 200, 255
Adams, John Quincy, 109, 134
Amos, John, 195
Andrews, Julie, 103
Armstrong, Louis, 209
Arnold, Roseanne, 149
Austen, Jane, 85

B-52's, The, 187
Bacall, Lauren, 128
Bachman, Randy, 196
Bachman-Turner Overdrive, 196
Bacon, Francis, 92
Ball, Lucille, 121
Batista y Zaldívar, Fulgencio, 124
Beatles, The, 37
Beatty, Warren, 269
Ben & Jerry's, 160
Benatar, Pat, 41
Benchley, Peter, 13
Benny, Jack, 101
Berlin, Irving, 271
Bernhardt, Sarah, 237
Berry, Chuck, 75
Blank, Arthur, 176
Bogart, Humphrey, 22
Bolger, Ray, 214
Bono, Sonny, 80
Bowie, David, 129
Boy George, 239

Brando, Marlon, 105
Brontë, Charlotte, 60
Brooks, Garth, 119
Brown, Edmund, 171
Brown, Helen Gurley, 27
Brown, James, 207
Brynner, Yul, 28
Bunton, Emma, 97
Burns, George, 275
Bush, George W., 219

Cage, Nicholas, 139
Cagney, James, 55
Caine, Michael, 254
Campbell, Glen, 146
Capra, Frank, 266
Carey, Mariah, 165
Carnegie, Andrew, 82
Carrey, Jim, 148
Carter, Jimmy, 98
Cash, Johnny, 24
Cassidy, David, 107
Castro, Fidel, 124
Cerf, Christopher, 142
Cervantes, Miguel de, 258
Charrière, Henri "Papillon," 158
Cheever, John, 224
Chisholm, Melanie, 97
Clay, Henry, 134
Cleopatra, 268
Cleveland, Grover, 220
Clinton, Bill, 51

Clinton, Hillary Rodham, 277
Cobb, Lee J., 264
Cohen, Ben, 160
Cole, Natalie, 73
Columbus, Christopher, 64
Confucius, 118
Conrad, Charles, 42
Coolidge, Calvin, 38, 127
Cooper, Gary, 96
Cooper, James Fenimore, 116
Coppola, Francis Ford, 43
Cosby, Bill, 245
Costello, Elvis, 273
Costner, Kevin, 276
Couric, Katie, 177
Cox, James M., 127
Crawford, Joan, 267
Crosby, David, 123
Cruise, Tom, 16
Crystal, Billy, 95
Cukor, George, 137
Curtis, Tony, 186

Davies, Dave, 218
Davies, Ray, 218
Davis, Bette, 137
DeMille, Cecil B., 71
Dean, James, 151
Denver, John, 59
DeVito, Danny, 225
Dewhurst, Colleen, 35

Diamond, Neil, 259
Dickens, Charles, 188
Diddley, Bo, 254
Dietrich, Marlene, 223
Disney, Walt, 29
Domino's Pizza, 248
Dostoyevsky, Feodor, 122
Doubleday, 174
Douglas, Kirk, 86
Douglas, Stephen, 272
Dreiser, Theodore, 174
Dreyfuss, Richard, 40
Dylan, Bob, 167

Eastwood, Clint, 115
Ebsen, Buddy, 249
Edison, Thomas Alva, 162
Einstein, Albert, 203
Epstein, Brian, 222
Estefan, Gloria, 69

Federal Express, 202
Fiorina, Carly, 87
Fisher, Donald, 234
Fitzgerald, F. Scott, 180
Flynn, Errol, 172
Fonda, Henry, 83
Fonda, Jane, 45
Ford, Gerald, 145
Ford, Harrison, 193
Ford, Henry II, 150
Franklin, Benjamin, 166
Freud, Sigmund, 26
Friedan, Betty, 215

Gable, Clark, 210
Gallagher, Noel, 104

Gandhi, Mahatma, 228
Gap, The, 234
Garbo, Greta, 53
Gardner, Erle Stanley, 120
Garland, Judy, 47
Garner, James, 253
Gates, Bill, 62
Gibson, Debbie, 263
Gideon, Clarence Earl, 226
Ginsburg, Ruth Bader, 189
Gleason, Jackie, 90
Goldman, William, 126
Gould, Elliott, 188
Grable, Betty, 117
Grant, Cary, 11
Grant, Ulysses S., 17
Greenstreet, Sydney, 81
Grisham, John, 243
Groh, David, 214
Guess Who, The, 196
Guns N' Roses, 52

Hackman, Gene, 131
Hale, Alan, Jr., 30
Haley, Jack, 249
Halliwell, Geri, 97
Hamill, Mark, 63
Hammer, M. C., 156
Hammett, Dashiell, 79
Harding, Warren G., 127
Harrison, Benjamin, 220
Harrison, William Henry, 134
Harry, Deborah, 65
Hawking, Stephen, 144
Hawn, Goldie, 50

Henry, O., 25
Hepburn, Audrey, 103
Hewitt, Don, 99
Hewlett-Packard, 87
Hirsch, Judd, 164
Hitchcock, Alfred, 169
Hoffman, Abbie, 142
Hoffman, Dustin, 163
Home Depot, 176
Hudson, Rock, 21
Hynde, Chrissie, 58

Jackson, Andrew, 109, 134
Jacob, 112
Jagger, Mick, 191
James, Rick, 257
Jefferson, Thomas, 255
Joan of Arc, 19
Joel, Billy, 77
John, Elton, 229
Johnson, Donna, 168
Johnson, Lyndon, 238
Johnson, Samuel, 94
Jones, Davy, 190
Jones, James Earl, 78
Joplin, Janis, 233
Jordan, Michael, 19
Joseph, 100
Joyce, James, 170

Karloff, Boris, 251
Keats, John, 132
Kelly, Gene, 244
Kennedy, John F., 153, 171
King, Martin Luther, Jr., 39, 181

Kinkos, 240
Kinks, The, 218
Kroc, Ray, 216

Laemmle, Carl, 137
Lancaster, Burt, 206
Lauper, Cyndi, 31
Leah, 112
Leakey, Louis, 250
Leakey, Mary, 250
Lemmon, Jack, 84, 108
Lenin, Vladimir, 274
Lennon, John, 161
Leno, Jay, 91
Leo X, Pope, 32
Leonardo da Vinci, 140
Letterman, David, 34
Lewis, Jerry, 208
Lewis, Jerry Lee, 231
Lincoln, Abraham, 272
Lindbergh, Charles, 38
Lindsay, John, 157
Little Richard, 138
Louis, Joe, 242
Love, Courtney, 57
Loy, Myrna, 78
Lucas, George, 43
Luther, Martin, 32

Madison, James, 260
Madonna, 201
Malcolm X, 197
Mandela, Nelson, 102
Manilow, Barry, 141
Mao Tse-tung, 68
Marcus, Bernard, 176

Marshall, Garry, 232
Martin, Dean, 199
Marx, Karl, 48
McDonald's, 216
McLaren, Malcolm, 58
McQueen, Steve, 178
Midler, Bette, 159
Monaghan, Thomas, 248
Monkees, the, 66, 123, 190, 217
Monroe, Marilyn, 9, 61
Moore, Mary Tyler, 34
Moses, 236
Murphy, Audie, 246

Nasser, Gamal Abdel, 76
Nelson, Willie, 179
Newhart, Bob, 154
Newman, Paul, 108
Nicholson, Jack, 66
Nilsson, Harry, 183
Nixon, Richard, 13, 145, 171
Nolte, Nick, 63

O'Brien, Conan, 194
O'Connor, Carroll, 30
O'Connor, Sinead, 192
O'Donnell, Rosie, 143
O'Neal, Ryan, 18
Oppenheimer, Robert J., 230
Orfalea, Paul, 240
Osbourne, Ozzy, 93
Owens, Jesse, 62

Pacino, Al, 182
Paige, Satchel, 113

Papillon, 160
Parks, Rosa, 181
Penn, William, 247
Philbin, Regis, 72
Picasso, Pablo, 265
Pierson, Kate, 187
Poe, Edgar Allan, 20
Polk, James, 134
Ponce de Léon, Juan, 184
Presley, Elvis, 89
Pryor, Richard, 262
Ptolemy, 268

Rachel, 112
Ramones, The, 213
Reagan, Ronald, 145
Redding, Otis, 261
Reynolds, Burt, 33
Robertson, Cliff, 108
Roosevelt, Franklin Delano, 127
Roosevelt, Theodore, 36
Rose, Axl, 52
Rowe, Dick, 37
Russell, Jane, 84
Ruth, Babe, 185

Schneider, Fred, 187
Schulz, Charles, 168
Schwartz, Sherwood, 131
Schwarzenegger, Arnold, 70
Seinfeld, Jerry, 56
Seuss, Dr., 10
Sex Pistols, The, 241

Shepherd, Cybill, 155
Simmons, Gene, 135
Sinatra, Frank, 14
Smith, Fred, 202
Spencer, Diana, 13
Spice Girls, The, 97
Spielberg, Steven, 212
Springsteen, Bruce, 46
Stallone, Sylvester, 70
Stanwyck, Barbara, 133
Stevenson, Adlai, 44
Stradlin, Izzy, 52
Streisand, Barbra, 12
Strickland, Keith, 187
Swift, Jonathan, 49

Tarkenton, Fran, 130
Taylor, James, 205
Taylor, Zachary, 134
Thackeray, William, 252

Thomas, Dylan, 110
Thurber, James, 270
Tomlin, Lily, 211
Tork, Peter, 217
Torn, Rip, 221
Townshend, Pete, 152
Travolta, John, 175
Trotsky, Leon, 106
Turner, C. F., 196

Valentino, Rudolph, 78, 267
Van Dyke, Dick, 235
Van Halen, 135
Verne, Jules, 114
Vonnegut, Kurt, Jr., 15

Waits, Tom, 67
Wal-Mart, 256
Walters, Barbara, 99
Walton, Sam, 256

Warhol, Andy, 61
Washington, George, 88, 200
Waters, Muddy, 125
Welch, Raquel, 173
West, Adam, 194
West, Mae, 147
Westheimer, Dr. Ruth, 23
White, Barry, 227
Who, The, 152
Wilder, Gene, 136
Williams, Cindy, 111
Williams, Robin, 74
Wilson, Cindy, 187
Wilson, Ricky, 187
Woolworth, F. W., 198
Wright, Orville, 54

Yeltsin, Boris, 204

Zanuck, Darryl, 9

Acknowledgments

I am deeply grateful to Terry Adams, Jeremy Solomon, and Peggy Freudenthal. Above all, all my love to Debbie for helping me create my two greatest successes in life—Ashley and Julia.

About the Author

Joey Green was nearly expelled from Cornell University for selling fake football programs at the 1979 Cornell-Yale Homecoming game. He was thrown off *National Lampoon* for writing an article in Rolling Stone on why *National Lampoon* wasn't funny anymore. This book was rejected by twelve publishing houses.

Joey Green is the author of nineteen books, including *Polish Your Furniture with Panty Hose* and *Wash Your Hair with Whipped Cream*. He has appeared on *The Tonight Show with Jay Leno*, *The Rosie O'Donnell Show*, *Late Night with Conan O'Brien*, *Today*, and *Good Morning, America*, and he has been profiled in the *New York Times*, *USA Today*, and *People*.